HEART OF THE STORM

BOOK 2 OF THE STORM CYCLE

RK KING

Stormwalker
MEDIA

ebook ISBN: 978-0-9958965-6-7

Paperback ISBN: 978-0-9958965-7-4

Cover art by J Caleb Design - www.jcalebdesign.com

For Erin
Dream Free, Bright Eyes

There are many worlds. We Shall See Them All.

Join the RK King Readers' Tribe and receive a FREE short story, as well as take part in occasional giveaways, updates, behind-the-scenes info, and much more! Join today at rkkingwrites.com

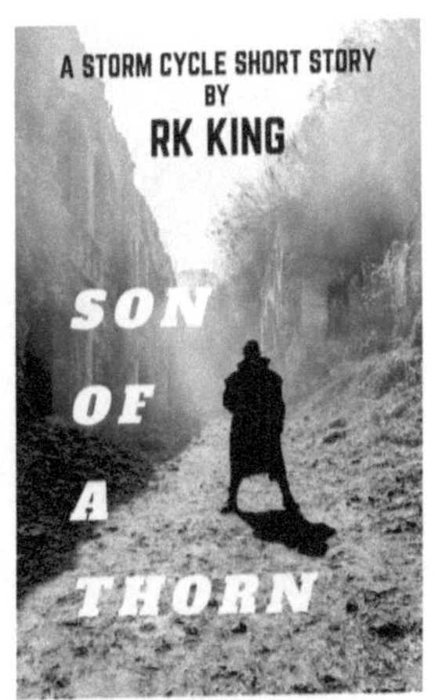

Son Of A Thorn is a short story prequel to
Eye Of The Storm and The Storm Cycle.
Receive it FREE by clicking the image
and joining up with the RK King Readers'
Tribe at www.rkkingwrites.com

PROLOGUE

ARE YOU ALIVE?

Yes. Yes, or so it thinks. It can feel the slow rhythm of its chest, the motion of air entering and escaping its lungs. But instead of the quiet thumping of its heart, the labored whirring of wheels and spindles slowly rouse its body to consciousness.

Pain is the first sensation it feels, spreading like viscous liquid from its chest to the tips of its toes and fingers. At least it knows it is alive; death would be the absence of feeling, would it not?

Can you see?

Yes, it can. The light seeps through the gaps of its eyelids like burning gold, expanding itself throughout its vision. Whenever it opens its eyes, it flinches and jerks away from the light's intensity. Its eyes are not accustomed to the brightness, colors, the surroundings, everything. It's as if it hasn't used them for a long while, if ever.

Something is not right. As it tries to move, waves of pain wash over it, and so it stops moving entirely. It can't reach its eyes -- it's bound, it can't break free. Its eyelids close like a shutter of a camera, eyes seeing the ceiling through an imaginary lens.

Why can't you move?

A touch of leather. Straps bind its wrists to the table. It realizes its whole body is bound and shackled, though for what reason it cannot fathom. It knows the leather straps are paper in the face of its strength, and yet it does not break them. The pain across its whole being is what keeps it from doing such a reckless thing.

No. Now is not the right time.

So many questions, but none that it can voice out to this room. Who is it going to ask, anyway, in this barren room of light and mechanical vibrations? Who is it going to call for help, for release against its bonds?

It tries to speak, it does not hear the sound of its voice. Rather, it feels the vibration and hears the shuddering of gears deep within.

Why is it this way? How do you hear?

Its ears; they should be on the sides of its head. That's where they are supposed to be...right? Why does it not feel the curved lobes of its ears or the ear canal where the sound should pass through? And despite the absence of ears, why does it hear even the most minuscule pops of its joints or the sound of the room's air colliding against itself?

It cannot move its hands to reach the sides of its head, to check for the lobes that should be there. Instead, it has an inkling of the things within its head -- sensors. Just odd-shaped things that capture the sound as needed.

It gathers the courage to speak, despite the obstruction of wires and the mechanism which allows it to generate a voice. "Hello?" Its voice is smooth and almost metallic, monotone and manufactured as a mimicry of real voice. "Is someone there?"

No one answers.

But it *spoke*. It made sound. Though it was nothing like it had expected, it now knew it had a voice. It was someone, or something, with a real existence.

But who's existence are you? When did it begin?

It realizes then that there are no memories of before. Where did it come from?

What is happening?

"Hello?" it tries again.

And again, nothing.

It is alone. It wonders if it's always been alone.

There is a routine. It's a routine which repeats as clockwork.

It wakes, and questions its presence in the room. It feels the mechanisms of itself, and the hard slab of the table it rests on. It notes the restraints. It notes the empty shadowed corners of the room, the stillness of the air. It's familiar with the darkness. And it calls out, always to no avail. Then a cyclical forced sleep.

The routine repeats, always on time, never changing. It would've gone mad if not for the pain in its body every day. The pain reminds it that yes, it's alive. Yes, this is real.

And it still doesn't understand.

Why are you here?

The same questions, so many times, but never any answer. It can only fathom it's here because it's here, because it's here, *because it's here*. It wars against the silence, against the unknown.

How did you get here?

The question plagues it again. The question implies it had a life beforehand -- a world beyond these four walls. But what if it didn't? What if this is all there was?

Do you know what you are?

Yes -- no...No it does not. It does not know. It does not. But, doesn't it?

Do you want to find out?

No...no, not yet.

The routine begins to end again, and the light in its eyes fade. As the darkness claimed it once more, knowing the cycle would repeat at a later time, it had just a moment for one last thought.

Learn what you are.

CHAPTER ONE

AN EXPLOSION ROCKED the rugged landscape, sputtering clouds of dust and stone in its wake. A group of nomads then emerged from the cloud and weaved through the barrage, avoiding the chaos as their lives depended on it. Another explosion hit the sparse grasslands at their right side, causing some members of the group to trip and fall. A young woman wearing a short cloak and hood turned to the others and shouted, "Left! Veer left!"

The group did as instructed before a massive boulder fell from the sky, blasting a crater into the ground where they had just passed. Dirt and rocks obscured their line of vision. The group would've descended into a coughing fit if not for the scarfs and masks protecting them.

Once the cloud was finally clear, a man ran up next to her. His face, like the rest of them, was covered with bandaging and goggles to create a mask, and a hood to block out the elements. He had a rifle slung across his back. His arms and hands were wrapped in bloodied bandages and strips of cloth.

"It's getting closer!" he told her. "Nemo, we have to move!"

In the distance, Nemo could see the outline of the massive shape that had been pursuing them; a beast towered twenty feet high with a muscular frame covered in coarse dark fur. It had six legs, all capped with steel-hard hooves that easily flattened houses and cracked the ground as it walked, and a large flat nose which dripped with mucus. Six-foot long tusks jutted from its jaws, covered in gore which provided a horrible stench of rotting flesh and decay. Each step from the beast caused a resounding boom that matched the blast of the rocks.

Without warning, the beast lunged and snapped its jaws at the nearest member of the group. The runner screamed as he shot his pistol, futilely trying to damage the beast, but each bullet bounced off the creature's skull. Before the beast could grab the man by its jaws, another runner, a woman, tackled the man to the side and both of them fell to the ground. The giant animal rushed just past them as they hit the ground hard.

"Jeez Hobbes! Be more careful!" the woman yelled as she pulled her goggles aside to glare at him.

Hobbes looked up to the familiar eyes of the young woman who'd chastised him. Her face was caked with dirt and grime and dust, but her eyes still reflected her steely resolve. He simply grinned. "Thank you, my dear Larina. I'm glad to know you've got my back."

Larina couldn't help but roll her eyes and turn back to the creature.

The creature made another attempt to attack the nomads, this time targeting Hobbes and Larina specifically. The two scrambled, making a run for it as the beast chased them down. Another member of the group, a young man wrapped in a poncho and scarf, appeared from the dust clouds, twin revolvers in hand. He showered the creature with bullets at its most vital areas: Chest, throat, face, chest again.

But once again, the bullets ricocheted against the beast's thick flesh, and the three of them were forced to roll on the ground to evade the creature's stomps.

Hobbes and Larina began to force themselves to their feet, while the newcomer approached and offered his hands, pulling them up. He spoke through his scarf. "That went well."

"Less talking, more running" Larina huffed, and the three of them continued on with the rest of the group.

The beast circled back and approached the group again. Nemo stood her ground, reaching for the holster on her thigh with her free hand. The taller man next to her pulled his rifle from his back. He was joined by another young man on Nemo's other side also bearing a rifle.

"Aiden, Deacon," Nemo spoke as she regarded her two companions. "On my mark."

Aiden and Deacon both aimed, waiting for the beast's familiar form to emerge from the dust.

When the beast lunged at them with its open jaws, Nemo shouted: "Now!"

Flashes of bullets rained down on the creature, puncturing both of its eyes and causing it to come to a thrashing halt. Nemo and the two men ran to their left as the creature stumbled and crashed, now vulnerable to attacks on the ground. Its sensitive underbelly was just within their reach.

That was her cue.

Nemo swiftly drew her pistol from its holster and fired at the beast's vulnerable belly. The creature gave a fitful cry and collapsed, sundering the surrounding grounds. Its six legs gave their final spasms and then went still.

When the dust settled, Nemo looked at the split ground and huge craters in front of her. She winced. This amount of destruction hadn't been part of their plan.

As the two others re-slung their rifles, Deacon placed a hand on her shoulder.

"You did good, Nemo. Mission accomplished."

Nemo nodded. She felt more at ease with the validation from her comrade. "Thank you, Onyx."

Deacon, the man also known to the Stormwalkers as Onyx, shook his head. "It's Deacon now, remember?"

Nemo pulled her scarf away to reveal a smile on her sleek features. "Sorry. I'm used to the old ways, you know?"

Deacon chuckled, waving his hands in dismissal. "I know all too well. But still, here, right now, you did good."

Aiden nodded. "Yeah, we helped people here today. Thanks to you."

"And I'm glad for that," Nemo said. "But I feel bad for the thing. How long has it roamed this land, its home? Did we really have the right to come here and end it?"

"Can't be helped," Deacon said. He pulled off his mask, revealing the weathered face of a middle-aged man. "We are Stormwalkers, and the burden that title carries can't be ignored. The oath we've made will always call for some sacrifice."

Nemo pursed her lips. She knew it was true, but it didn't make the situation any less harsh than it already was.

Meanwhile, the other three nomads of their group were catching up.

Aiden briefly waved at them before turning back to Nemo. "Think of the lives we've just saved. How many people live in that camp? A few hundred? We've fought to give them another day to find Safe Harbor."

They were right of course, Nemo knew. Safe Harbor was the reason they were out in this world, bringing aid to all they could find.

Despite growing up in the region they now referred to as Safe Harbor -- an ancient complex from the time of the Storm-makers, when flying ships and technological wonders still existed; a place that bore the memory of its past through a symbol repeatedly displayed around it; NASA -- and often taking steps into the Storm as a fledgling Stormwalker, it wasn't until her time with Aiden and the others that her life had gained real meaning.

It had all been for Aiden and the other Pathfinders, a test of their worthiness to Stormwalker life. Her mysterious appearance before the Pathfinders, their willingness to search for a better home, and the following journey into the Storm that had all been orchestrated by Deacon, Aiden's father, to push their strength and bolster the Stormwalker population.

The Stormwalkers had doubted him but Onyx- or Deacon as the Pathfinders knew him- had believed in Aiden. And so he and Nemo had tested them.

The journey had been harsh, but those who'd survived had passed the test and found their place in a massive world they'd never dreamed of.

The Pathfinders, in constant conflict with other tribes like the Eagles and the Dogs, had been starving in an ever-dwindling eye of the Storm that surrounded them. They had no knowledge of the outside world. But those who agreed to try, and of those the ones who'd survived, came to learn the truth.

There was more than one Storm.

It had been a harsh truth, one that Nemo had disliked seeing on Aiden's face the day he'd learned how things were. He had been through so much, lost many friends and had proven his worth so much more, only to learn the journey was just beginning. But Aiden and her other friends had taken the challenge. Their only choice was to continue with the path forged ahead.

And so they had become Stormwalkers. They now traveled the Storms in search of the beleaguered and the trapped. They brought hope to the hopeless, and showed them a piece of the world they could feel safe and sound and at ease in. The population of Safe Harbor grew.

Nemo nodded again. She didn't have to like every step they took, but she was fine with resigning to the fact it was all for the greater good. They had indeed helped others this day, an entire tribe of people whose daily lives had been in constant threat of a dangerous animal.

Nemo's thoughts returned to her as Hobbes pulled off his hood to reveal a shorter, wiry young man with a mop of hair. He reached and shook her hand.

"Great shooting," Hobbes said. "That big beastie almost took a chunk out of me back there."

Larina and the young man with the poncho chuckled.

When Nemo had first met Hobbes he'd seemed, despite his actual age, like a child. Always quick to make a joke, he'd taken everything so very lightly. It was something that had both infuriated her and filled her with joy, especially during times when their cause had seemed precariously close to failure. But their cause had also tempered him. Hobbes' once child-like persona had hardened, and he'd grown into a capable fighter. Sure, he still had the occasional quip stashed away ready to be used, and she was glad for it, but she found she could rely on him much more now.

Larina pulled her mask aside and delivered a playful punch to Hobbes' shoulder. "Wasn't just her, you know. I recall having to literally knock your ass out of that trouble."

Nemo smiled. Perhaps Larina had something to do with Hobbes' development. One of the few survivors of the Thorn tribe, Larina had faced incredible hardship in the initial journey through the Storm, and she'd proven herself by it. Larina had fully dedicated herself to the mission and it showed the most when she had battled against the rogue Stormwalker called Skarn. Though she had barely survived the encounter, her combat skills were extensive and had only improved since then. When it involved hand-to-hand combat, Nemo trusted no one more than Larina. It was a trust that had proven beneficial more than once during the journeys since. Hobbes had been infatuated with Larina from the start, and though cold to his affections at first, the Thorn girl eventually warmed up to him. They'd grown closer in the following times, becoming often inseparable even.

Sometimes Nemo envied their flighty closeness. It was something she wasn't sure she had with Aiden. What her and Aiden had was... well, different. What had been something real, something tangible, had over time morphed into something... else. Perhaps it was the result of the trials. Perhaps it was Aiden growing into his leadership role. Maybe it was Nemo, herself. She had no answer, not at the moment anyway.

Her thoughts were pulled from her when the young man in the poncho unwrapped his scarf and draped it over his own shoulder. "I gather youd'a made a tiny snack" he said to Hobbes. "Not much meat on those bones to make a meal of anything."

"Hobbes is wiry," Larina agreed with a smirk. "But he's got muscle where it counts, Gord."

Hobbes grinned.

Clad in his signature scarf and poncho, Gord gave off a distinctive look. He sported a grown beard which encircled his jaw and chin like a patch of trimmed grass. He had a larger build than the likes of Hobbes or Aiden, due to his harsh life in these grasslands they were now traveling.

Gord raised his hands in defense. "I surrender. Not gonna risk the wrath of the wee one's lady upon me."

Nemo suddenly found herself surrounded by the embracing arms of Aiden.

"Wow!" Aiden laughed. "I'm so proud of you! Did everyone see that? Ruby knows how to get it done!"

Ruby. Nemo sighed at the name. True, Ruby was her Stormwalker namesake, one gifted to her as a toddler. But hardly anyone called her that these days, mostly due to her own insistence. Unlike Deacon's willingness to shed the Stormwalker moniker of Onyx, she much preferred the name of Nemo.

It had not been an intended name though. She'd had no idea it was the name of the airplane Aiden had found her in. But when he'd remembered the plane's call-sign and chosen to pass said call-sign onto the then-unknown young woman, she was quick to adapt to it. She identified with the name Nemo much more than Ruby.

Despite that nice memory, Nemo shrugged Aiden aside. His arms slid away, which brought a look of discomfort to his face. He attempted to take her hand in his, but Nemo skirted away from that as well. *Not the time*, she thought to herself.

She was about to state as much when Deacon raised his hand and pointed to the distance. From the horizon, Nemo could see the silhouettes of a group of people steadily approaching them.

The group's leader, a middle-aged man with a patchy red

beard, fiddled with his hands before him as he addressed the nomads. "Great Stormwalkers. Please accept our deepest gratitude. Many of our people have lost their lives to the beast, and today you rescued us from its grasp."

Deacon shook his head. "When we entered this Storm and found your village within its eye, we offered our help. Simple as that. Gratitude isn't needed."

"Still," the village leader nodded. "The beast is dead. The demon haunts us no longer."

He, and the other villagers, bowed their heads in relief and reverence.

"It was no demon," Nemo muttered under her breath. "It was an animal living its life. That's all." *Why was it so difficult to understand that?*

But her words made the rugged villagers become uncomfortable, and Deacon was quick to intercept. "Regardless, its path and your peoples' could not co-exist. Sometimes, such is the way of this world."

The elder nodded in agreement, "We have had to rely on Gord all these months to keep that beast at bay. We've been very proud of him. He has an incredible aim."

"We got to see as much with our own eyes," Larina said. "Where'd you learn to shoot like that, Gord?"

"'Yer skills get tested when 'yer on your own out here," Gord said. "But it wasn't enough. I'm glad y'all joined me in the effort. Thanks for the help."

Aiden nodded and looked back to the elder. "And now your people have the freedom to choose. You can live your life in peace here in the Eye, moving with the Storm. Or, you can take the journey to Safe Harbor. We've shown the way. For once, your path is clear. You have that choice now."

The village leader carefully regarded the whole Stormwalker group. "We do have that choice now, thanks to you. And we're grateful." He glanced toward his fellow villagers, then back to the nomads. "We shall discuss the matter further, but I'm confident Safe Harbor will be in at least some of our futures."

Deacon shook the man's hand. "Then I look forward to meeting you again. Dream free."

The villagers nodded their thanks a final time and headed back to their camp. Once they were gone, Hobbes turned to Aiden and Deacon. "Your story is pretty much scripted now, huh?"

"Our only story is one of freedom, Hobbes," Nemo said. "A story we'll keep telling to all those we find."

"What y'all are doing is amazing," Gord said. "All this time, I had no idea there was a safe place to aim for."

"You're more than welcome there as well," Deacon said.

"Maybe," Gord replied. "But for now I think I'll stick with y'all, if you'll have me. I wanna see more of what's out there, you know?"

"I think I can speak for us all," Nemo said. "You've proven yourself today. You are more than welcome to join us."

"But you're not a true Stormwalker yet," Hobbes winked. "That comes later."

"To the next Storm then?" Larina quipped.

Nemo nodded.

"Well alright," Gord chuckled and, with a bit of flair, wrapped his scarf back around his face. "Maybe we'll find some more critters out there. I can always use some more target practice." He made shooting sounds as he mimed firing his pistols with his fingers.

Nemo pondered over that. She wondered if they'd ever find a

Storm with a peaceful Eye for once. Outside of Safe Harbor, they had not yet found any peace in this world. The Storms made sure of that.

The Stormwalkers readied themselves and ventured forth for the next Storm. Their mission continued ever forward.

CHAPTER TWO

THE TREK WAS NOT EASY.

Upon exiting the Storm that held the villagers and the great beast, the Stormwalkers found themselves beset by a transition zone. Hail the size of adult human hands hammered across the plains, creating craters across the desert and tearing apart any living structure that dared to stand upright in this weather. The group huddled near each other, covering themselves with their armor-plated vests and bags to avoid getting hit by the hail.

"We must face it," said Deacon. "There is no other way!"

He pointed ahead, and the group could indeed spot the distant wall of another Storm. The surface of the wall glimmered with swirling patterns of dust and debris.

"Great," Hobbes complained. "It just *had* to exist outside of a freak hailstorm!"

Gord laughed and slapped Hobbes on the shoulder. For someone who's spent most of his life in one place, he didn't seem freaked out by this whole phenomenon. "You worry too much! This is my first ride outside my own Eye. Do I look scared?"

Hobbes grimaced. "Did I say I was scared?"

"You say many things, little man," Gord replied with a grin before wrapping his scarf around his face.

"Well I ain't saying that!" Hobbes faced the oncoming hail, but soon glanced to Larina. "*Do* I look scared?"

Larina shrugged and grinned. "Don't worry. You're big and strong to me."

Hobbes frowned. "Not helping. Fine! Let's do this."

The group pushed onward, with Aiden taking up the lead. He gathered their surroundings and surmised that these lands were yet to be tread, regardless of the number of Storms to pass over through the years. In the distance, he saw a wide plain of the barren grasslands, with an occasional shallow lake bed or lagoon, long-since dried up of natural life. The lake beds were now being filled by the hail, stacking up on each other like grains of sand in a jar. As the group trekked over the land, the environment gradually shifted to a thick canopy of woods, which shielded them from the onslaught of the hail. Instead, the hail softened to a cool rain, and the group halted at the trees as the ancient ground began to weave into itself.

Aiden stared ahead into the thickening forest. He could already feel the damp air that emanated from within, but couldn't see quite far ahead -- with every inch into the forest, the woods grew darker and dimmer.

"Swamp," Deacon said, noticing Aiden's stare. "There'll be a lot of life in there. Lifeforms that would be sheltered from the harshness of the Storms outside."

"So, in other words," Aiden realized, "Let's be careful."

"Again," Hobbes whined. "I've had enough big meat-eating monsters for a while."

"Although," Gord spoke up. "There might be a village or two in there. Kinda like how you found my people hiding in the last Storm."

"Gord's right," Larina said. "We can't skip this site. There might be people who need help."

Hobbes eyed Larina harshly. "Well sure. I just wish we had a better idea before walking knee-deep in dangerous swamps."

"You'll be fine," Aiden said. Then he turned to his group. "We all will."

I hope, he thought.

The Stormwalkers entered the swamp. They were greeted by the tall weeds and reeds that grew in this muddy place, tangling their ankles and dirtying their gear. Their pace slowed immensely, and not simply because of the soft ground underneath them. They had to be careful. If something attacked them now, they wouldn't be able to react quick enough.

It didn't take long for Aiden to begin questioning their decision.

It was mostly due to the air -- heavy and overbearing, like attempting to breathe through a syrupy soup. As the group traveled, Aiden could feel the heavy air as he tried to breathe. Soon, his hair began to stick to his scalp as his skin slicked with sweat. Aiden wished for nothing more than to remove his gear and clothing, and he assumed the rest of the group were suffering too.

"Remind me why we chose this way," Nemo rasped at his side. She also sauntered along with little power behind her steps, and she kept wiping her brow with her sleeve.

"The same as always," Aiden said simply. Talking took too much of his breath. "To help."

Gord, who'd long since unwrapped his scarf from his face,

shook the canteen on his belt. "Don't know about the rest of y'all but I'm running low on the thirsty stuff."

Aiden nodded. "Same here. Good thing we're surrounded by water."

"No. Look," Deacon said, pointing, and the rest of them halted .

The group understood immediately. Where the water trickled along in sorry excuses for streams rested the rotting remains of numerous animal life. Different types of bats, lizards, rodents and other small creatures floated their way along the surface, making a trail of corpses along the water.

Larina gagged while Gord threw up what little was left in his stomach.

"Damn glad I removed my scarf earlier," he sputtered, spitting the remains of his vomit.

"Okay," Aiden coughed at the stench of decay and the swamp. "No fresh water for a while."

"But we can't be sure when there will be clean water," Hobbes said. "This is getting risky."

"What else can we do?" Aiden asked. "Turn back?"

"Well, that's what I would do! At least we'll find some water without the creepy things for added flavor."

Aiden shook his head. "This swamp is uncharted. No Stormwalkers have been here. We don't know if there are people here who need our help."

"And we don't know if there's *nobody* out here either," Hobbes argued. "Is the risk worth it?"

Aiden paused. Isn't that why they were here? The discovery of knowledge doesn't come without risks, and that's what the Stormwalker trials had prepared them for.

Aiden shook his head. "We've seen what's happening to the

world around us. We can't ignore it now. People are out there, struggling and dying, without any knowledge that there was a better life waiting for them if they only knew where to go. Can we really turn away?"

Hobbes waved his hands around them. "I understand, alright! But maybe what we're looking for is not here," Hobbes said. "Is this how things always gonna be, Aiden? Are we devoting our entire lives to this, without any concern of what's going to happen to us? This… this might be suicide!"

Aiden glanced to Deacon, then to Nemo, and finally back to Hobbes. "Remember the trials?"

Hobbes hesitantly nodded. "I do. Vividly."

"Against all odds, we found our way- no, fought our way to safety. We found the way out."

"We did."

"And do you believe that others deserve the same chance?"

"Yes. They do."

"And that means something," Aiden said. "You full-well understand what it means to be a Stormwalker."

"I'm not saying that I don't," Hobbes said. "I'm saying that this unnecessary risk that we're doing right now is, well, unnecessary."

Aiden growled. "Everything we do is necessary!"

"We should vote," Larina interjected, sensing the uneasy tension in the group. "See who wants to push ahead, and who wants to fall back."

Aiden shook his head. "We don't have time for that! The more we argue, the longer that others could be suffering."

"Could be, Aiden," Hobbes said. "Could be. We're tired. We're hungry. We are not at our best. If something popped out of the trees right now we'd be screwed!" He looked Aiden straight in the eyes and spoke with finality. "We need rest."

"We can rest once we find -" But then something caught Aiden's ear. Something... familiar. "Wait. Do you hear that?"

The group paused. They listened.

The breeze whistled through the trees; branches rustled across the canopy. Dead leaves fluttered on the ground, some dropping onto the water while others stuck on the sticky swampland floor. The sky rumbled above them and the smell of ozone filled the air. Aiden heard every breath and movement of his teammates. And amidst their breathing, Aiden could hear something else.

It was something faint and subtle, something hiding between the surrounding sounds of the swamp and the distant sounds of the Storm.

It wasn't just any white noise. It was something coherent, something with a design to it.

He heard whispers.

He couldn't discern the specific words. They were too faint. But it was definitely speech.

And it was something he was sure he'd heard before.

"There!" Aiden said. "Hear it?"

The group focused on the Swamp, before the Storm, to that delicate place in between. And then, one by one, they heard it.

"Please," Aiden continued. "Tell me you hear it."

"Yes, Aiden," Deacon said. "I hear it."

"There are people out there," Gord scanned the swamp. "They can't be that far from here."

The Stormwalkers nodded as one.

"Well," Larina said. "That settles that. Now we know someone is out here."

"Right," Hobbes sighed. "Fine. No more arguing. Let's do this. But which way?"

Aiden listened. Now that the sound was their focus, he followed its source. He looked one way, where he heard the creaking and rustling of the trees. Looking at the other way, he could only hear the small bugs and animals creeping through the dense foliage. And then, finally, Aiden looked straight ahead. He stared intently into the deep swamp, and he focused on the noises from that direction. It was faint and distant, but he could hear the whispers, stronger, more defined.

Before, he'd been confident. Now, he was positive. "We go West."

"Are you certain?" Deacon asked.

"I am. They're out here, somewhere."

Hobbes closed his eyes and listened. "He's right. Let's go."

The Stormwalkers advanced. As their approach narrowed, the sounds of the voices grew and hardened into a measurable presence. Soon, Hobbes fell into Aiden's pace as they walked side by side.

"Sorry for that, back there. I'm just worried, okay?"

"I get it," Aiden said. "You're looking out for the group. I appreciate that. But we gotta follow this through. I'm sure of it now."

"I wasn't sure at first either," Hobbes nodded. "It wasn't clear enough. But now, I'm sure too."

"Sure of what?" asked Gord, who was walking closely behind them.

"You weren't there," Nemo said. "We've heard these voices before, haven't we Aiden?"

Aiden nodded. "No mistaking it now. During our

Stormwalker trial, we encountered these voices. They've spoken to us before."

"Very good," Deacon said. "You're right. There must be another transmission spot ahead."

"Transmission?" Gord asked, confused. "I'm hearin' it, but got no knowin' what it is. What are ya'll going on about?"

But before Aiden could continue his story, the Stormwalkers emerged from the thickness of the swamp's trees. Ahead of them was a clearing which opened up to a small hill covered in grass and ferns. On top of the hill was a small building made of grey cobblestones and a steeped roof. The stone walls were beaten and weathered with age, covered in many years' growth of moss and ivy. The foundation, which seemed very old, stood defiantly against the advancements of the surrounding swampland, a holdover against natural forces.

"You want an answer, Gord?" Aiden asked as he scanned his surroundings. "Listen."

"We are here," a voice echoed down to them from within the building. "We exist. We were many, soon few. Find us. Help us. This message repeats."

"What was that?" Gord asked. "A recorded message?"

"We don't know," Deacon answered. "Remember what I said the first time we encountered this message. There are more mysteries than can ever be solved, hidden within the Storms."

"We came here to find people," Aiden said. "Maybe with this message we'll find them."

Aiden and Deacon began to climb the hill, while the rest of the group trailed behind them. The voice continued to relay its message like a broken record.

"We exist. We were many, soon few. Find us. Help us. This message repeats," the voice again echoed out to them.

Sheer determination propelled Aiden forward, shoving his feelings of caution down to nothing. He quickened his pace and passed Deacon, who called him to slow down. Aiden was already in front of the building and inspecting the single, simple front door when Deacon arrived. Aiden traced his fingers on the door's surface.

"What now?" Hobbes panted as the others arrived. "Do we knock?"

"We exist," the voice repeated, almost as if answering. "We were many, soon few. Find us. Help us. This message repeats."

"Why is it repeating its message like that?" Gord asked.

Ignoring the rest of the group, Aiden twisted the doorknob and found it unlocked. He then took a breath before he eased the door open, allowing the door to creak eerily across the hilltop. Slowly, Aiden stepped inside.

The room inside the building had no signs of life. Grey wallpaper was peeling off the walls, revealing the grey concrete underneath. The floor was adorned with layers of dust and gave a loud creak when Aiden stepped forward. A single broken light bulb dangled in the immediate center of the room which did not matter much as the room was still softly illuminated by a row of humming machines against the far wall. Buttons and screens blinked and flashed different colored lights and a series of monitors fizzled with static signals. The screens all displayed the same fizzled image, that of a figure in shadow filmed from the waist up. Their face was hidden through a censored blurring of the footage.

"We exist. We were many, soon few," the unknown person on the screen spoke in a flat, direct tone. "Find us. Help us. This message repeats."

"Well I'll be," Gord said in awe. "Who is he?"

"No idea," Aiden said. "Not even sure if it *is* a he. The voice sounds weird, altered somehow."

"Just like the last time," Hobbes said.

"We exist," the message repeated again. It did indeed sound flat, almost not real. "We were many, soon few. Find us. Help us. This message repeats."

"Faoin Storm, níl sé seo ag cabhrú leis," Nemo cursed in her own Stormwalker tongue.

It had taken some time for Aiden to learn some of the dialect, and he'd still barely scratched the surface. But he knew Nemo's tone of frustration when he heard it.

"I know," he muttered. "They've never given any details. Where they are? Who they are? Just this vague message."

"And yet, they are asking for help," Larina said. "Find us, help us, right? How do we do that, then?"

The message finished another cycle.

"I'd hoped to find something more," Aiden said as he stared at the mysterious machines and their unknown subject. "I'm sorry, everyone. This is a dead end."

The message repeated again, but this time Gord stepped forward. "Ya'll missin' something? I hear it. Don't you?"

"There aren't any more clues, Gord," Hobbes said. "You never heard it the first time. This one's the same."

"I may notta' heard it before," Gord said. "But I'm hearin' it now. Listen!"

The message repeated, but didn't change. The group was confused.

"Still the same," Hobbes said, "Nothing new, again."

Gord shook his head. "Not that part. Listen!"

The message repeated again.

"What are you talking about?" Larina asked, sounding frustrated.

But Aiden looked at Gord and thought, What are you on to, Gord?

"Listen now!" Gord exclaimed. "No, not now. There, now!"

The message repeated again, and was followed by a moment of silence. Then it repeated again.

And Aiden knew.

"Well I'll be," Aiden said in an imitation of Gord.

"What?" Hobbes asked.

"Don't listen to the message," Aiden said, smiling. "It's not the message, it's what's beyond the message. In between."

The message repeated. There was one second of silence before it repeated again.

"Now listen again," Aiden said.

They did. There was a three-second gap before the message started again.

"Again!"

When the group did so, they noticed that the message had a five second gap before repeating again.

"The breaks between the messages have different lengths," Larina whispered.

Hobbes' eyes widened. "You think the other station was the same?"

"I think so," Aiden said. "We just didn't notice."

"Okay," Hobbes agreed. "So we have different lengths of breaks in between the messages themselves. So what?"

"So I'd reckon the same group of numbers that make up those breaks will repeat themselves too," Gord said. "What would a particular set of repeating numbers mean, on a map perhaps?"

Deacon laughed. "We've had coordinates handed to us all along."

"Well okay," Aiden said, smiling. "Let's do some math. Someone pull out a map."

CHAPTER THREE

THE STORMWALKERS STUMBLED upon a coordinate system when they arranged the spaces between the repeating transmission. The sequence of numbers revealed an undiscovered area of swampland large enough to potentially house some inhabitants.

And to think, Nemo thought, *we likely wouldn't have realized it without Gord.*

Gord looked quite pleased with himself as the group left the transmission shack. "Yep," he said. "I reckon y'all are pretty pleased I chose to tag along."

Larina laughed. "Careful, Gord. Don't go getting a big head now."

"Why, never," Gord gasped. "Or I'll eat my scarf."

Nemo smirked, and looked back to the map in Aiden's hands. "On the right course?"

"Yes. About another day's walk West," he replied. He squinted his eyes and held it closer to his face. "Or two days."

Nemo chuckled. "Okay, Mister Pathfinder-turned-Stormwalker. Lead the way."

Nemo watched Aiden's shoulders sink a little. He went quiet and simply stared ahead.

Good one, Ruby, Nemo thought to herself. *Such an idiot.*

Aiden sighed.

"I'm sorry," Nemo said. "I realize the Pathfinders are kind of a question mark, still."

In the process of becoming Stormwalkers, passing the trials and escaping the Storm, Aiden and the others were forced to leave the rest of the tribes behind.

Nemo knew Aiden considered the tribes of the Eye as his home. The Pathfinders, the Eagles, the Thorns and the Dogs all existed in constant conflict and distraction for generations. Their way of life had become normalized to the point that the very idea of a world outside their Eye was heresy. Most had turned down the Stormwalkers when they presented a chance to escape their dwindling existence. Those who took a chance with the Storm and survived the trials of the maelstrom went on to become Stormwalkers themselves. However, there were those who had chosen to remain behind.

"We left them behind," Aiden said finally. "They doubted the mission, but do they deserve to suffer because of it?"

"They chose to stay," Nemo reminded him.

"When we left, the Eye was shrinking. The only remaining space would soon be out on open water. There wasn't much time left for them."

"The Pathfinders were aware, Aiden. Many still made their choice."

"And the other tribes? You think Jorus would have allowed the Eagles to learn their world was vanishing? Not everyone in the Eye got to make a choice."

"You're putting too much of that on yourself," Nemo said

delicately. "The lives of those who stayed are not your burden to bear."

Aiden paused. "I'm not so sure."

"Aiden," Nemo reasoned. "Think of what the Stormwalkers stand for. We travel the Storms, seeking survivors to help, yes?"

Aiden nodded.

"Maybe other Stormwalkers had made their way back into your Eye," she continued. "There may be Pathfinders, or any of the other tribes, waiting at Safe Harbor right now."

"You don't know," Aiden muttered.

"You're right, I don't. That's why I said may be. I said it that way because I hold hope."

"Hope. Is that all?"

"Hope is a lot. Hope got us through the trials. Hope helped us overcome so many obstacles. I'd say hope is what drives everything we do now."

Aiden paused to consider her point, a look of recognition forming on his face.

"You might be right," he admitted.

"Well, yeah," she smiled.

"I still think about them. A lot."

"Of course you do. Because you're a great person."

"She's right," Deacon added from further back. He stayed behind them, his face hidden loosely under his hood, his signature goggles covering his eyes. "We've no idea what's become of the tribes. We have no idea how Jonah is doing."

"Jonah," Aiden said.

Nemo could tell Aiden was worrying about his grandfather. The old leader of the Pathfinders had remained to lead those who'd chosen to stay in the Eye.

Deacon continued. "But it doesn't change what we do now.

Perhaps we will be able to return to the Eye in the near future. Perhaps we won't. Either way, in the meantime, we have a mission."

Nemo observed conflict in Aiden's eyes. It was a conflict which hadn't changed since the trials and would likely remain until they learned what had happened to the Pathfinders.

Or, she realized, *what if they had to return to the Eye themselves?*

She didn't like the idea of returning, since the Stormwalker trials had been established due to the dwindling resources and space in that Eye. She doubted there'd be much of an Eye left and dreaded the idea of Aiden coming to that realization.

And then she noticed Aiden's eyes focus as he seemed to come to a decision.

"Yes," he said. "You're right. We don't know what's become of the Pathfinders, or any of the tribes. But we have something else that is for certain. We have a signal, a definite source we can follow, which should lead us to someone who's out here in this swamp."

"They're not the Pathfinders," Nemo agreed. "But they are people, survivors who we can lead out of here. Let's focus on that."

Aiden nodded. "We'll show them a new path, right? It's what we do."

Nemo liked the smile that formed on Aiden's face and the halfhearted attempt he made to keep it.

Aiden's resolve is weakening, she thought. Can we fix this?

Hobbes forced a cough that drew their attention. "In about a day's time we'll have some new faces to greet, right? Let's make sure they feel welcome. Safe Harbor awaits!"

Nemo glanced back at Aiden and saw a renewed focus.

Don't lose focus, Aiden , she thought. *We need you. Despite everything else, we need you.*

She *was* worried though. She wondered, as long as the question of the Pathfinders' fate remained, how long would that focus last?

CHAPTER FOUR

AIDEN'S PREDICTION of the distance of their journey seemed accurate as the sun began to set under the canopy of the swamp.

It could have been good news for the group but Larina was having none of it.

Her thoughts kept returning to the arguments of her fellow Stormwalkers. Aiden constantly needed to know what had become of their tribes, but Nemo reminded them to prioritize the mission, and Hobbes had to find ways to defuse the situation.

What's happening here? she asked herself. *I wish I knew what happened too, but if we keep arguing, does that mean we're coming apart?*

"The sun is setting," Deacon said. "We should stop for the night. Start early in the morning."

Right back on with the mission, she thought.

Larina's further thoughts were cut off when the group heard a sound. It began as rustling in the surrounding foliage, something that would have been easily mistaken for a small animal. But then sound became more hurried, as if a large herd was descending upon the swamp.

"Somethin' comin' our way," Gord muttered at Larina's side as he subtly drew his pistols.

She glanced quickly to her fellow Stormwalkers and noticed that they had drawn their weapons. She drew her spear and gripped it in her familiar stance as she went into position.

The sounds shifted. What had sounded like a careful stampede through the swampland changed to a manic press headed directly toward them. Trees creaked, branches snapped and the sound of water echoed around them. It was obvious they had been targeted by... something. And that something was almost upon them.

"Ready!" Deacon cried as he cocked his rifle.

The sound of the oncoming force suddenly stopped and the group tried to sense if anything what could be amiss. Silence blanketed the group as the sounds of chirping birds and buzzing insects had vanished. There was a stillness about the swamp that felt completely unnatural.

That stillness shattered, as featureless forms descended from the treetops. The unknown figures traveled from tree branch to tree branch as they escaped detection. The Stormwalkers then sensed their presence just as a glinting metal object flew and sunk into Gord's shoulder.

Gord yelped and dropped one of his revolvers. A dark figure slammed him into the wet ground when he tried to fire with his other hand. Hobbes tried to counter with his rifle, but the hooded assailant was faster than he. At that moment, Larina witnessed as the stranger's arm grasped the rifle, twisted it, and took the young Stormwalker off his feet.

She tried to track the stranger, but its cloak billowed and hid their features apart from a buzzing sound on the arm.

The stranger tossed Hobbes with ease and sent the young

Stormwalker careening into a tree. The attacker then turned to the group and raised its arm above its head. A cable shot from the stranger's forearm, high into the above foliage, and Larina observed the strangeness of the metal appendage. Small amounts of light glinted off the arm's metal surface as the stranger rose back into the treetops.

They're metal? Larina asked herself. *Are they even real?*

She realized that they were very real, though, when two more hooded attackers descended from the treetops. They hit the shallow swamp floor with similarly metallic legs and feet that hissed upon landing.

One thing was for certain; they were not friendly.

Deacon launched himself into an offensive stride, followed by Nemo and Aiden. The three Stormwalkers delivered strike after strike but most of the trio's attacks failed to land. The few that did had little effect. Aiden even recoiled in pain after smashing his fist against one of the stranger's chests. A loud clang resounded, alongside Aiden's cries as he shook his hand. The cloaked figure whirled around, knocked Aiden off balance, and smacked him into the swamp floor. The attacker raised its metallic leg with the intent on delivering a crushing blow.

"No!" Nemo tried to close the distance between them but got blocked by the other assailant. She was forced to defend herself as it managed to attack both her and Deacon in unison.

Larina launched herself against the stranger and felt her collarbone give way on impact. She hit the ground gasping and rolled away from the fallen foe. Her breath came out in short breaths as she gripped her spear on one knee.

Her enemy lurched in the mud and rose onto its feet staring down at the half-kneeling Larina.

Larina tried to see its face and barely made out the cold grey of something metal and the tiny glint of light where its eyes should be. Reflection off goggles, perhaps? The constant presence of the hood hindered her observations.

"What are you?" Larina asked.

The figure tilted its head in response. A mechanical hissing accompanied its movement as it stared at her. In a sudden and inhumanely fluid motion, her attacker spun around and grappled Nemo, who'd tried to sneak up from behind. Nemo was repeatedly struck with small, precise hand strikes until she collapsed onto the soggy swampland floor.

Larina had risen to her feet and glanced to her side where Deacon battled the other stranger.

He paced his strikes and used his superior height to his advantage. In between the Stormwalker's connected kicks, the metal arms of the stranger delivered hard-hitting strikes in kind. Deacon was driven lower and lower to the ground. The attacker grasped Deacon by his own cloak and lifted him high before bringing him back crashing into the muck.

Larina was furious. She turned back to the enemy before her as the figure reached for Nemo. Larina roared in anger and thrust her spear into the enemy's back. The attack briefly made contact, but her spear immediately skidded off to the side with a loud scraping sound.

She never got to process the thought as her attacker spun around and thrust its metallic hand towards her throat, causing her to drop her spear. The hand began choking her with inhuman strength.

No air, gotta breathe! It hurts! It hurts!

She thrashed against her opponent's arm, but the stranger didn't budge. It simply continued its dangerous grip on her neck. A furious scream roared on her left flank, and Nemo charged the cloaked figure with Larina's spear. Her attacks successfully connected but mirrored the same effects with Larina's earlier attempt.

Not armor, Larina thought through dimming consciousness. *They're made of metal...*

Still gripping Larina, their enemy turned on the spot and caught the spear with its free hand. There was an audible snap, and Larina saw through her fading vision that her spear had become no more. Nemo stood still and looked down at the remaining stub of the spear's wooden pole. While she was distracted, the metal attacker delivered a single-legged kick. The attack sent her flying into a tree and face-first into the mud.

Larina feebly grasped at her assailant's wrist, but the stranger paid no mind. She mustered the last of her strength and whispered, 'Nemo...'

Everything went black.

Nemo groggily rose to her knees, spitting out the mud of the swamp. She glanced around to start a head count. Everyone else was slowly regaining consciousness and accounted for.

Except for Larina.

Nemo spotted the broken pieces of Larina's spear in front of her. Another quick glance told her all she needed to know; that the metal attackers, and Larina, were gone.

CHAPTER FIVE

THERE WERE NO TRACKS, of course.

Despite their desperate attempts, the only sign the attacking strangers had ever been there was the disturbed mud and grass where the fight had occurred. Other than the tracks the Stormwalkers themselves had made during their arrival, no prints showed a path the enemies had taken to leave.

"Makes sense," Aiden said as he rubbed his head for the third time, trying to ward off the headache that had accompanied his reawakening. "They got here through the trees, so they left through the trees."

"And took Larina with them!" Hobbes said.

"They did," Deacon agreed. "But the question is why?"

"The why doesn't matter!" Hobbes said. "Let's just go after them!"

"And how you reckon we do that?" Gord asked. "You somehow see magical tracks in the air? 'Cuz I sure don't."

That silenced Hobbes. For the time being, at least, Aiden thought.

Nemo spoke up. "Why did they ambush us like that? Who were they?"

"More like *what* were they?" Aiden pondered. "Hitting that guy was like hitting a car door."

Deacon nodded. "Yes. Though they wore heavy cloaks and hoods, they fought with a skill I just couldn't match. They made no errors. Their technique was perfect. Too perfect."

"What do you mean?" Nemo asked.

"I'm not entirely sure," Deacon replied. "Not yet."

That's not like him, Aiden thought. He couldn't think of a time when he had seen his father in such a state of being unprepared. Whoever these strangers were, they caught Deacon off guard, and that worried Aiden. It worried him a lot.

"So that's it then," Hobbes said. Everyone turned to him. "The signal. The people on the other end of the signal. It was a waste. It was a trap, and we walked right into it. Now Larina is gone."

"What do we do?" Gord asked. "Hobbes ain't wrong to be miserable. How in the hells are we 'sposed to find Miss Larina?"

"I don't know," Deacon said. "I'm looking and looking and I can't find any trace to follow. Unless, maybe, in the trees."

They all stared upward.

Hobbes said, "Someone give me a lift!"

While Hobbes and Gord set to tree climbing, Nemo approached Aiden. "What are you thinking?"

Aiden sighed. "I'm thinking we're gonna get into those trees, we're not gonna find anything, and we're gonna be back where we started a few minutes ago."

Nemo glanced to Deacon, who was overseeing Hobbes' and Gord's efforts. "Deacon doesn't know what to do either. That's a first."

Aiden nodded.

"But," she continued, "what else are we gonna do? Abandon her?"

Aiden glanced to the surrounding trees, staring off in the direction they'd been headed before the ambush. He took a breath, and nodded. "Actually, yes."

Hobbes and Gord paused upon hearing him, ceased their climbing, and looked down at the others. Deacon also regarded Aiden silently.

"I don't understand," Nemo said.

Aiden asked the whole group, "What was the mission?"

"We've been over this!" Hobbes growled. "It was a trap! Screw the mission, there's no one out here!"

"We don't know that," Aiden said. "And until we can be sure, the first step of the Stormwalkers' mission is finding those who need help."

"Larina needs help!"

"Of course," Aiden reasoned. "I'd agree to follow her too, if we had any sign to follow! We just don't. But what we do have is a signal we can follow."

"Yeah. He's right," Gord said. "Even if it was a trap, don't y'all think the source of the transmission is where we might find her?"

The whole group remained silent for a time. Hobbes glared at each one of them, but when no other defense came he jumped back down to the swamp floor. He stomped his way to Aiden.

"Don't you dare," Hobbes pointed a finger at Aiden. "Don't you dare."

I'm sorry, my friend, Aiden thought. "We do a vote."

"Why are we acting like it's even a question?" Hobbes demanded. "She's in danger, we go find her!"

"Things aren't as easy as you're trying to make them."

"No!"

"We vote."

"I said no!"

"Enough!" Deacon said, making the two friends snap quiet. "Why are we here?"

They all stared at him, until, finally, Gord spoke. "The mission?"

Deacon shook his head. "Why are we here?" Then, as he indicated down at the ground, "Why are we right here, right now?"

What are you getting at? Aiden wondered.

Deacon sighed. "We are Stormwalkers. We are here, right now, in this place, because we have earned the right to be. We have been through everything the Storms can throw at us, and yet we stand here. As Stormwalkers, we have the mission to help those we find in the Storm, but what truly defines us is what the Storm has molded us into. We are fighters. We will not bend, we will not break, no matter how strong the Storm rages. We stand, and we carry onward. We could take a vote, true. But the result would be pointless. This is because, as Stormwalkers, we continue the fight. We continue the journey, no matter what."

Hobbes stared at them with a gaping mouth. He was fuming.

"I'm sorry, Hobbes. I am," Aiden said. "But we need to carry on, as we've done in every Storm we've been in. We may find Larina at the source of the transmission, we don't know. But an aimless search will not help her in any way, and would be a waste of time and our Stormwalker journey. We continue onward."

Hobbes said nothing. Instead, he simply turned and headed in their original direction.

Gord and Nemo both regarded him, and followed.

Deacon nodded. "That was difficult. But it was the right decision."

"I hope Hobbes can see that, some day," Aiden muttered.

The continued journey through the swamp was one done in silence. No one spoke. No one dared. Hobbes led the pack, far ahead, in a stomping manner that showed he no longer cared who or what in the swamp became aware of his presence.

But maybe that's the point, Aiden thought. Hoping to get caught, hoping to be brought to Larina?

"Aiden," Nemo then said as she approached. "How are you?"

"I'm fine. Why?"

She regarded him a moment. "Just making sure."

"Like I told Deacon, I believe in what we're doing. There is a cost to that. I hope we find Larina where we're going, I really do. But the transmission comes first."

"You'll tell me when something doesn't sit right with you, yeah?"

Aiden paused. Nemo had been getting colder and colder toward him lately. He could tell that what they once had seemed to have disappeared after the Stormwalker trials. Despite the fact she'd hid the truth from them, Aiden had chosen not to hold that against her. Was she still feeling like she had betrayed them? Was it something else? Every time he tried to get close to her again, he'd only been greeted with a wall of dismissal. So why now with the concern? "Sure, Nemo. Of course."

Nemo seemed like she was about to say something more, until a strange groaning sound filled the area.

The group froze.

They heard the groan again, a sort of grinding sound that managed to echo itself through the trees.

As Aiden glanced from side to side, he noticed the swamp water about their feet, and although they had been standing still for a few moments, was rippling heavily.

"What is that?" Hobbes turned around to face the group. "Almost sounds like someone's driving a truck through the swamp."

The groaning got louder. Aiden could hear a constant rattling that accompanied the continuous groan. Soon the noise was loud enough to drown out the swamp sounds around them.

"Then it's the biggest damn truck I ever heard of!" Gord yelled, his voice barely overpowering the thrum.

And then the trees exploded before them.

The Stormwalkers dove in every direction, avoiding the shattered limbs and splintered chunks of the demolished trees as they soared past. Then, as they each worked to regain their footing they looked to the newly created hole in the swamp ahead, and to the arrived terror upon them.

A massive metal hulk of a machine, it moved like a truck, but instead of wheels it was carried forward by large treads that devastated the swamp floor beneath it. Dirt and sludge got pulverized, flattened, ground up, and flung outward continually beneath the behemoth's treads. The paneling that covered the vehicle was uniformly slanted at all angles, giving it the appearance of an animal's shell. The metal surfaces of the machine's exterior glistened, slick with the swamp water it forced its way through.

As the Stormwalkers stared in awe, they quickly realized they were also staring at a series of machine guns mounted on the front of the vehicle. And as the firearms freely swung forward to bear on them, they realized the armored tank's intentions with dismal clarity.

"Run!" Deacon cried.

The guns opened fire. Lines in the swamp water formed, traveling all around and chasing the Stormwalkers as bullets flew and impacted at their feet. The tank continued to roll forward, the guns wheeling and pivoting on its front to follow its targets as they ran. The barrels of the weapons kept track of its targets, never missing a step directly after them.

"Move! Move!" Nemo ordered as she ducked and dodged in the swamp.

"We're not losing it!" Hobbes warned.

Aiden felt the whizzing of a bullet right next to his face, and felt the warmth of his ear's blood pooling down the side. He ducked again just in time for a second bullet to miss his skull by inches.

The tank continued to barrel its way forward.

As he ran, Gord pulled his revolvers and fired. His shots hit the hull of the tank, and ricocheted off without effect. "Wha'?!"

How do we fight that? Aiden thought. Then his eyes went wide as Nemo, running for her life, whipped around as a bullet hit her shoulder. She fell to the ankle-deep water, and immediately tried to scramble backward as the tank bore down upon her. Fighting to regain her footing, the slickness of the swamp floor kept tripping her up. She ignored her bleeding shoulder as she slid backward, but to no avail.

The treads of the tank were moments from crushing Nemo, when Aiden witnessed another thing. He stared in awe as the cloaked form of Deacon leaped from a nearby tree. His father hit the top of the tank, hard, collapsing to his knees. He began hammering his fists on the tank's surface, taking hold of a handle to what appeared to be a hatch.

The tank inched closer to Nemo. She could no longer roll away to either side, the tank's enormous bulk overbearing her path no matter which way she faced.

"No!" Aiden screamed, realizing he wouldn't make the distance in time.

Deacon fought against the sealed hatch. His grip on the wheel wavered, but he twisted again and, roaring with anger, he used every ounce of reserve Stormwalker strength he still held. The wheel snapped, and Deacon ripped the hatch door open.

The tank slowed, and stopped. Nemo was practically under the tank's treads. She swiftly crawled free, gasping and frantic as she rose back to her feet.

Aiden reached her, tending to her bleeding shoulder. "You okay?"

She nodded, shaken but standing.

Gord gave a perplexed whistle, and the Stormwalkers looked to where he was staring at the top of the tank.

Deacon stood, arm stretched out and gripping the shoulder of the tank's driver, who he had evidently pulled out from within the tank's protective inner sanctum. But the Stormwalkers weren't interested in Deacon. They were interested in the man he had restrained.

If they could call it a man, that was.

As the captive darted his head back and forth to regard each of the Stormwalkers, multiple things became apparent. First, the man's face, while displaying a sense of surprise, was muddled in a pallid shade of an almost grey color. His skin also had cracks running all over, like weathered porcelain. Second, although his skin had its sickly dullness, the man's eyes shone with an immensely bright ring of blue while the rest of the eye was shadowed in total blackness. And third, as the man turned his head to face his captor, Deacon, they all saw a gaping hole in the back of the man's head.

This guy should be dead, Aiden thought.

A bluish fluid seeped from the head wound, and the Stormwalkers were able to see a sense of movement within, something whirring and clicking, something that moved with precision, all while that blue fluid seeped and flowed throughout, almost like the oil of an engine would.

"Mechanical," Aiden said, and to the others, "He's a machine!"

And then the machine spoke.

CHAPTER SIX

*E*RROR*. Fault located, upper hatch. Prepare counter-measures.*

Optical sensors rotated upward even before the ceiling's hatch ripped open. Despite the cramped space becoming harshly filled with ambient light of the outside swamp, the pilot needed no time to adjust its eyesight to take in the form of the intruder peering down at it. Within nanoseconds the pilot registered what it saw, cross-referenced with similar categorized potential threats, and judged the stranger to be an obstacle to overcome. It swiftly raised its hand, brandishing a pistol pointed at the attacker. But the target was surprisingly fast, and reached downward to grasp the gun's barrel and rip it away just as the pilot realized what was happening.

Unexpected fault. Target speed unexpected. Error. Alter counter-measures.

The attacker, clad in a cloak, goggles and bandaging, hit the pilot over the head with the butt of the gun, which only resulted in a clang. The pilot jolted its arm upward to grab the man"s arm. It squeezed, and the stranger growled in pain. But instead of surrendering or retreating, the intruder gripped the pilot's forearm as well. Then he squeezed.

Error. Target strength unexpected. External forearm chassis compromised. Redirect current-

But then the pilot got yanked upward and out of the tank.

The pilot was shorter than its captor, which caused it to hang by the shoulder from its attacker's outstretched hand. As it took in the scene before it, it darted its sights from one stranger to the next, then coming to rest, its head turned, to glare at its captor.

"Validity of mission compromised," the pilot spoke, its voice droning along in a single dull tone. "Hostile activity prevents unit from action. Processing..."

"Whoa," one stranger, the shortest male, said as he stared. "Look at its face when it talks. I can see gears in its mouth."

"Affirmative," the pilot said. "Vocal instruments required to project sound via radio channels aboard vehicle. Vocal instruments in unit at optimal condition."

It noticed one of the females' shoulders was bleeding rather profusely, but she didn't seem to give it another thought. Her eyes, like everyone else's, were fixed on the mechanical man that had just pulled out of the hatch.

Another young male stepped forward, a drop of blood from his ear landing on his shoulder. With a stern face, he looked the driver in the eye, as if it was trying to instill fear into a machine.

"Who are you?" the male asked firmly, getting right into the machine's face.

"Uka Five-Two-Zero-Zero," the machine man replied.

"Maybe the better question would be *what* are you?" the short male whispered to the hurt female.

"Uka Five-Two-Zero-Zero is an early model unit charged with patrolling the City perimeter, and to engage potential threats" Uka 5200 answered, without a hint of emotion in his voice.

"So you realize you almost ran me over?" the female asked, a hint of anxiety still in her voice.

Uka 5200 swiveled his head around to meet her eyes with his own blue-black ones. His face revealed no expression. "Yes."

The short male suddenly closed the gap between himself and Uka 5200, getting right into the machine man's face. "You're a little too slick about almost murdering my friends, Uka Five-Two-Zero-Zero," he spat. "Why don't we show you what that's like?"

"Hobbes, please," the tall man holding Uka replied. "We have many questions, and it seems he will only offer up information he is directly asked about. So until we have our questions answered, no one will be harming the robot." The others, though visibly disgruntled, did not contradict the man's word. They all turned their attention back to Uka, waiting to hear what else he might have to say. "So, let me make sure we understand you, Uka,"

"Uka Five-Two-Zero-Zero," the machine reiterated.

"Right, of course. Uka Five-Two-Zero-Zero."

"And to be precise, this unit is not a robot."

"I've read about robots," Uka's captor replied. "Machines created by the Stormmakers."

The group of people looked on at Uka in a state of awe.

"This unit is an android."

"An android? What's the difference?"

"Robots were autonomous machines," Uka said. "Generally produced to aid in manufacture, resource acquisition, and other dangerous endeavors not safe for organics. Robots were-are... rarely designed in anthropocentric dimensions. Ideally, instead they are designed for what menial task they are allotted. Androids are designed for... error... other reasons."

The tall man appeared to ponder this reply for a minute. "Your job was to patrol the perimeter, but what for?"

"Patrolling units are posted at specific points around the perimeter of the city to protect the inhabitants that reside within," Uka 5200 stated.

"City?" the man with a beard perked up. "He sayin' there's a city further in there?"

"Interesting," the tall man murmured, as if in deep thought. "I'm thinking that Uka Five-Two-Zero-Zero here was never meant to leave the protection of the tank. It seems as though he was not designed to keep any kind of secrets, like what his job might actually be. If a real enemy threat had wandered in here, he would likely blow the cover of the city and lead the enemies right to their targets."

"So you're saying there's a whole city of people-er-units like you? And you're one of the most important members protecting your city?" the wounded female asked.

"Perhaps. It is this unit's job to control the weapons and deter enemies and targets from reaching the city walls that lie within."

"Well then, you failed your mission," the tall man stated. "We stopped your weapon and now have you. What's to stop us from infiltrating your city?"

"It is clear that this unit did not fulfill its job to the expectations attributed to it. This unit should not be able to be stopped by any creature. But as you can see, this unit is damaged and in desperate need of repairs," Uka 5200 pointed to the back of his head at the large hole, blue filmy liquid still seeping out. "This unit cannot leave its post and run the risk of enemies getting into the city, so this unit fought with its damages and still failed."

Uka 5200 hung his head, as if in disappointment. The others seemed astonished with Uka's matter-of-factness.

"What kind of repairs do you require?" the young man, possibly their leader, asked. The rest of the crew turned to look at him. None of them looked thrilled at the question.

"This unit requires a full system reboot before it can answer that question with complete confidence and accuracy," Uka 5200 replied.

"Can we assist with that?" he asked.

"This unit will need to be taken back to the city and inspected," Uka raised his head, no longer hanging it in shame.

"Why don't we escort you to the city and help you find the repairs you need?" the human offered, earning exasperated looks from his team. "Perhaps you can help us with something we're searching for in exchange for getting you back to your city safely, and fixing you up."

"This unit cannot make any guarantees, but this unit is sure we can ask Gar Four-Three for assistance. That unit is much more capable of answering questions that are less direct," Uka admitted.

"Well, that's good news, at least," the female muttered. "Maybe this Gar can help us with the signal."

"Gar Four-Three," Uka 5200 remarked.

"Or finding Larina," the short male added, still seemingly upset by something.

"Uka Five-Two-Zero-Zero, are you able to lead us to your city, so we can get you the repairs you need?" the tall man asked of the android.

"Yes, this unit's GPS system is still running. Please follow." Uka 5200 straightened up and zoomed forward out of the tall man's grip. He led the way into the swamp without hesitation.

Uka looked back only once, to see the group of humans staring at each other in a state of confusion before finally following.

Uka 5200 moved quickly through the swampy terrain, much faster than the rest of the crew, who traipsed on as fast as they could through the marsh. Their boots kept getting stuck in the mud of the swamp, and their feet made horrible squishing sounds with every step. Uka 5200 never once looked back to ensure that his followers were close behind, so it was up to them to make sure they didn't lose the machine man.

"Hey, Uka?" Nemo called ahead, out of breath.

"Uka Five-Two-Zero-Zero," he corrected.

"Right. Could you maybe slow down? Move at a slower pace? Some of us have actual lungs in our bodies that can't take the speed you're moving at," she gasped.

"This unit could move at a slower speed, but this unit was under the impression we were in a hurry to fix the damages in this unit's head," Uka said.

"Right, well, that's all fine, but we're having a much harder time getting through the swamp than you are."

It was clear that Nemo was irritated, which lightened Aiden's mood. "Uka Five-Two-Zero-Zero, please continue. But if you could move a little slower, it would be much appreciated by the rest of us."

"We have almost arrived," Uka announced. "You will soon meet Gar Four-Three and this unit will be back to optimal capacity."

"Fantastic," Nemo grunted.

It was not long before the muck and mud they trudged

through turned dry. The crew was able to move more easily along the dirt now that they were beyond the swampy terrain.

"How much further?" Hobbes asked between haggard breaths.

The group approached a ledge, and the ground dipped steeply to reveal a sprawling metropolis of steel and metal. Aiden's eyes widened as he took in the state of the city. Steel and stone structures that once resembled buildings had long ago rusted and decayed.

A large river, probably once a majestic flow of clean water but now a fetid, languid body of green swamp, snaked its way along next to and through parts of the city. Close to where they stood was a massive bridge of metal that crossed its way over the river and into the city across the water. Aiden spotted the remains of a second parallel bridge that had collapsed into the river. That bridge's legs remained as massive pillars jutting from the water, but the bridge itself, likely the exact twin of the intact one, had crumbled and sunk beneath the waves some time ago.

"This way," Uka 5200 said and continued toward the bridge.

As they reached the edge of the river and prepared to cross the bridge, Nemo paused and looked toward a weather-beaten sign that leaned haphazardly on a rusted pole. The painted surface of the sign had mostly been stripped away by time, but the name of the bridge could still just barely be read; CRESCENT CITY CONNECTION.

"Welcome," Uka 5200 pointed toward the city. "Welcome to the Crescent City."

The android led the Stormwalkers onto the bridge and toward the once-great city that care forgot.

The crossing of the bridge took quite some time, with the group continually being instructed by Uka to turn this way and that way, avoiding the often broken holes in the bridge's paved surface. For most of the journey Aiden kept staring down into the swampy water of the river below. He imagined the animal life that might be hidden down there, and wondered at how different that same animal life may have been when the river had been a clearer, cleaner version of itself in the distant past. These thoughts got pushed aside though as they finally reached the opposite side of the river and approached the city.

The unique architecture of the city's buildings were noticeable. Single, double and even triple-storied structures lined the broken and dusty streets. Terraces and pillars adorned many of the buildings. Most of these ancient buildings were long since stripped of their vitality, but some still held traces of the various colors they bore once upon a time. There were a few taller buildings as well, skyscrapers and towers that once held important use. But they were few compared to the vastly more numerous shorter dwellings that lined most of the city's streets and pathways. Abundant greenery had covered much of the city as well, some buildings appearing completely inaccessible due to the growth.

The Stormwalkers were quick to notice citizens entering and exiting the habitable buildings. They also quickly realized that the citizens were all machines, just like their new friend Uka. Although the numerous citizens were focused on their own tasks at hand, the Stormwalkers found themselves the center of attention every time they entered a unit's peripheral vision. Regardless of what any particular individual was in the middle of, they instantly halted and watched or even followed the Stormwalkers. The androids appeared to be just as much in awe of the humans as the Stormwalkers were of the robot population.

One unit, a slim female-oriented specimen, even dropped the

tool belt it was carrying and approached Uka. "Uka Five-Two-Zero-Zero," the unit said. "What have you done?"

Uka blinked his black-blue eyes once. "Greetings Tru Four-Four-Nine. This unit is returning to base two-three-four for critical maintenance. Observe cranial damage this unit is currently sustaining."

Tru 449 blinked her own eyes once, staring at Uka's head damage. "This unit is referring to the lifeforms escorting Uka Five-Two-Zero-Zero. They are...organic."

Uka nodded. "Affirmative. This unit instructed these humans to follow this unit to The Crescent City. This unit has promised the human group aid in relocating one of their own."

"There are more humans?"

"We are missing our friend, yes," Deacon answered. "We've been told someone in this city can help us."

Tru remained silent then. Uka eventually stepped past her and beckoned for the Stormwalkers to follow. "This unit apologizes. Organics are a rarity here. This unit recommends getting used to similar reactions from the population."

They then passed a large building made of stonework, its exterior walls crumbled with the years. The front facade was highlighted by a series of stone columns that were made to look like they were holding up part of the front of the structure, but Aiden was pretty sure they were decorative only. A spherical object stood atop a lone column to the side of the entrance. The object itself was a bluish sphere, with the word HARRAH'S set upon it. The entire object probably served some purpose long ago, but Aiden could not tell what that would have been. Glancing into the building's entrance as they passed, more androids of various sizes moved around inside. What they were up to, Aiden couldn't understand.

"Please follow," Uka 5200 stated. The android roved on, deep into the heart of the city, the crew following right on his heels.

Aiden tried to take the sights in and understand the city as they moved onward.

"Where exactly are we going?" Hobbes asked.

"Gar Four-Three resides in the mechanics suite of base two-three-four, which is just further down this street," Uka pointed to a tall building in the distance. "You can see it from here."

They knew what Uka was referring to immediately. In the distance down the road stood a massive structure. Circular, it was only a few stories high, so not a building that reached for the sky like the ones the Stormwalkers had encountered in their travels. This building was instead shaped like a massive wheel, with a diameter so large they could only speculate but were sure it took up much of the space of the city's center itself. The outer walls of the building rose at a slight angle, then concave in their middle, to then reach further up in the opposite direction until reaching the faded-white dome of a roof. The middle concave gave the appearance that some mighty Stormgod had reached down and pinched the building at its center to create the interesting shape of its surface. As the group made their approach, they then spotted a sign above the large entrance to the structure. Much of the sign had fallen and vanished over time, it's initial portion long gone. The second half of the name remained though in rusted letters; SUPERDOME.

"Who would build a structure like that, and why?" Hobbes asked.

"Unknown," Uka said. "This city was desolate when adopted by our initial parameters. Our makers... long gone now... established an infrastructure to allow us to self-regulate. This 'superdome', with its large interior space as you'll soon see, was adopted into base Two-Three-Four, a mechanical operations lab. We do not fathom its original usage. Today, this unit hopes its cranial damage can be repaired within."

"Hopes?" Nemo asked. "You mean it might not work?"

"Possible outcome. It is not certain what the precise problem is inside this unit's cranial chassis. Without that knowledge, this unit cannot say if it is able to be fixed by Gar Four-Three," Uka 5200 replied.

"Comforting," Nemo sighed.

"Nemo, trust the android," Deacon said. "This is the best chance he has to fix his head, and we need his help to find the signal. We must follow this through. Uka Five-Two-Zero-Zero, could we stop for a moment?"

"Why must we stop?" Uka 5200 asked.

"We came across your armored vehicle because we were searching for the source of a signal we heard. A sound of voices--whispers, of sorts--we were trying to find the source of the voices. It was a transmission, like a radio signal. We're hoping it will lead us to find our friend Larina who was taken."

"If there is a radio signal that is audible to human ears, Gar Four-Three will know how to find the source. Finding Gar Four-Three will be your best option."

"Thank you. Please, take us there," Deacon said, pondering their next move.

At this, the android led on, approaching the superdome -- Base 234. Aiden felt a pang of hope; that Gar 43 would be able to help them find the signal and lead them to Larina. The guilt of not following after her was stinging in his chest, and he knew Hobbes was unbearably livid. He could only hope the decision he made was for the best.

Uka 5200 approached the building and slid the door open to allow the group through. They came upon a set of rusted and dilapidated stairs, but Uka 5200 did not hesitate to climb. Aiden shook his head, but followed. When he turned around, only Deacon had climbed after him.

"Are yeh sure it's safe?" Gord asked, uncertainly.

"Of course. If it was unsafe, this unit would not utilize it," Uka 5200 replied. That seemed to be enough for Gord, and the rest of them followed suit. It took several minutes before reaching doors that opened to a large room that looked much like a laboratory of sorts. There were fifty or more androids moving about, going about their tasks. "Follow me, please," Uka 5200 instructed shortly.

Aiden began to wonder if the request to follow was because Uka didn't want them poking around in the lab at any of the work. It heightened his curiosity, but he followed orders.

"Gar Four-Three, this unit apologizes for showing up unannounced, but this unit has large damages that need repairs," Uka 5200 asked of an android that looked much like the others.

Though similar to every other android present, Gar 43 seemed to bear an air of command that the other androids simply followed. Gar 43 gave orders and pointed in directions, only stopping when Uka 5200 approached. The machine leader blinked his photo-receptor eyes as he took on the visitors.

"Uka Five-Two-Zero-Zero, why have you brought organics with you? Was it not your job to protect the perimeter of the city from threats?" Gar 43 asked.

"The organics were scanned and determined not to be a threat," Uka 5200 stated. "They are looking for a radio signal and this unit believed there may be a way to help them."

Gar 43 stared silently for a few moments, unblinking,

perhaps processing this new information. "Very well, if you would all follow me, this unit will need to tend to Uka Five-Two-Zero-Zero's damages. Then we can discuss the matter of your radio signal."

"Thank you," Deacon said. "We apologize to your city for our presence."

Gar 43 said nothing in reply, and instead grabbed and ripped Uka 5200's head from his body.

CHAPTER SEVEN

NEMO GASPED as the android removed Uka 5200's head from his body, but then reminded herself that, as machines, the removal of the head from the body was probably not quite as catastrophic as it would be for her fellow Stormwalkers. Androids were not really alive, right? At least, that's what she had to reason with herself.

"Is that safe? I mean, can he still live--er--survive without it?" she asked.

"Affirmative," Gar 43 replied. "In matters of cranial damage, it is much easier to work on the repairs when the head is removed from the body. Do not worry; Uka Five-Two-Zero-Zero feels no pain. This unit activated Uka Five-Two-Zero-Zero's stasis switch before removing the cranium. This unit will turn Uka Five-Two-zero-Zero back on once the damage is repaired."

Another android, with the visage of a tall woman with the same cracked skin, approached with a device in her hand. She tapped the device's screen a few times while speaking. "Pardon me, Gar Four-Three, but we were working on calibrating the

Linx models for application to Cerberus, and we are all stuck on-
-wait a moment. Are these...humans? Here?"

More androids approached seeking advice from Gar 43, but ultimately got distracted by Nemo and her group of friends. Upon hearing their excitement, Nemo took a step back as the group of machines rapidly approached. She couldn't help but expect this to be an ambush.

"Nemo," Deacon said firmly. His arm shot out behind her, preventing her from taking any further steps backward. "Notice their tone. They are not a threat to us. At least not at the moment... They are curious. When do you think is the last time they've seen any human being?"

The thought hadn't crossed Nemo's mind, but Deacon was right, as usual. The androids now mingled with the humans. The humans were under scrutiny by the robots; the men of metal came dangerously close, peering at each human individually, taking in the minor details and differences of each person. Many of the androids focused on Gord's beard, as well as Hobbes's freckles.

"How peculiar," one android remarked.

"Why don't they all have these intriguing spots?" another asked.

"They are so...different from each other," a third said.

As an android approached Nemo to analyze her features, she panicked. She ducked under its arm and dodged around the android to keep her distance. Aiden gave her a quizzical look.

"Listen, I know they haven't seen a human in ages, or possibly ever, but I don't need them getting all up close okay?" she reasoned to Aiden.

"I suppose that's a fair point," Aiden smirked.

"Units, please," Gar 43 called out. "Give the humans some room to breathe."

"Do they not have enough oxygen when we are this close? I assure you, we will not take up any extra oxygen. We do not require oxygen to function," the tall female android said.

"What I mean is please give them some room. Humans need space to feel comfortable. We want them to feel welcome here, so let us focus on their needs," Gar 43 clarified. "This unit is almost finished with Uka Five-Two-Zero-Zero and then we can give our new visitors a tour of the facility."

After another few minutes, Gar 43 was reattaching Uka 5200's head to his body. He flipped a switch, reactivating Uka 5200 who was now able to move and speak as he had before.

"How do your functions operate now, Uka Five-two-Zero-Zero?" Gar 43 asked.

Uka probed around his own head with his fingers for a moment, noting the spot where the gap in his cranium was. "Despite the remaining cosmetic damage, this unit is believed to be at one hundred percent working capacity. Thank you for your help Gar Four-Three."

Gar 43 then turned to the humans. "Now, you said you were looking for some kind of radio signal, correct?"

"Yes, actually," Aiden replied. "We were entering the swamp when we heard the voices. At first, we thought there might be more people, but the more we listened, we realized it was some sort of radio signal that was on a loop. We've been trying to find the source of the signal because we're hoping the source might also lead us to our friend. She was taken, and we're not sure where she might be," Aiden explained.

"Taken? By whom?" Gar 43 asked. "Are there more humans in the swamp lands?"

Nemo paused at this. She recalled the clear distinction of the attackers. Though they hid their faces and identities well, she more than felt their powerful strikes. Their armored limbs. The hissing sounds as they moved. No, something didn't sit well with her still, and she began to consider why.

"We don't know who they were," Deacon said. "But they fought well, and we are now missing a comrade."

"Well, let us take a tour of this base," Gar 43 said. "Our city does broadcast signals to the perimeter units within the swamps, so we must first address a possibility the radio signal you are searching for is being transmitted from this building. There is a transmitter on the top floor. This unit does not spend time up there, therefore uncertainty is present. Would you like this unit to take you there?"

"Yes, that would give us all some peace of mind, I think," Deacon said.

Gar 43 nodded his head once and then took off back through the laboratory they arrived through and into an elevator. Each of the members of the group piled into the elevator, and when Gar 43 pressed a button the car lurched upward. She felt as though she left her stomach behind back on the laboratory floor as the elevator car shot upward faster and faster.

Finally, the elevator shuddered to a halt, the doors slid open, and everyone began to file out onto the floor. Nemo looked around at what appeared to be an empty hall. A set of double doors at the end of the hallway lead to another room, full of unknowns.

"We are going to enter the room designated as the cockpit. There are only three other units working up here. They should be able to answer any questions you might have. This unit's hope is the information they hold will help you find your friend. Let us proceed," Gar 43 explained. He led the way through the empty hall and gently pushed open the double doors, exposing the cockpit.

As the group entered, three other androids worked intently on something. They seemed too caught up in their work to even recognize their visitors.

"Rev Two-Seven, these humans have some questions for you, if you could spare time for them. They are missing one of their own and are on a search to find the human," Gar 43 explained to one of the three androids. The receiving android did not look up from its work, but gave a slight nod in understanding. "Right then," Gar 43 continued. "This unit will leave you with your questions. If you find you need more help, this unit will be back in the laboratory below. It appears the Linx connection continues to need attention..."

"What is this 'Linx' you've mentioned before?" Hobbes asked.

But instead of answering, Gar 43 made his exit back to the elevator and disappeared. The group of humans stood in the cockpit, awkwardly waiting for the android--Rev 27--to finish and address them. After a few minutes, the android rose and approached the group.

"You have questions for this unit?" Rev 27 asked.

"Yes," Nemo said, rather impatiently. "Do you happen to broadcast a radio transmission that would reach all the way through the swamps?"

"Affirmative. There is one signal we broadcast continuously for those units patrolling the perimeter of the city. This unit can play it for you to see if it is the one you are looking for?"

"That would be great, thank you," Deacon cut in, stopping Nemo from possible further rude responses.

The android did not seem to recognize the difference between politeness and rudeness, however--or maybe it just didn't care. Either way, Rev 27 zoomed off to the control panel and pushed a few buttons before a sound began to echo throughout the cockpit.

Suddenly, the room began to fill with voices dictating coordinates and orders checking in, but they were certainly not the same voices they had experienced down by the swamps. Nemo's heart, initially swelled with hope and anxiety of getting somewhere, deflated as soon as the voices began.

"Was this the transmission you heard?" Rev 27 asked, dryly.

"No," Nemo's voice quavered. She was not quite near tears, but she was highly disappointed.

"This unit is sorry to hear that," Rev said.

The android had said it in a way that didn't sit well with Nemo. She could almost picture the android making the decision to outright lie to them. Could a machine even do that? What if it was programmed to? Nemo was frustrated. She didn't understand technology, all the relics of the Old World just seemed like a waste to her, but now they were being forced to go along with the whims of these mechanical...people. *It's not really sorry*, she thought to herself. *Why should it be?*

"This is the only transmission broadcasting far enough to reach into the swamps," Rev continued. "We don't want to create mixed signals for our androids on the front lines."

Nemo started at that. "You say this is the only signal that goes far enough to reach into the swamps. Are you telling us you do not broadcast out beyond the swamp lands? Out into the Storms, out into the world?"

"We do not," Rev 27 replied. "This unit believes your group are the first humans seen in decades. It is cataloged there are no signs of life outside the Storm beyond the swamp lands. It would be assumed your group came from the swamp, if not for your own words otherwise. There are no signals reaching further than the perimeters of the swamp."

"We appreciate you taking the time for us," Deacon said, coolly.

"Allow this unit to call up Uka five-two-Zero-Zero. This unit understands you are familiar with that particular unit? Uka Five-Two-Zero-Zero can take you on a tour of the building and help you get comfortable while you are here."

Rev 27 pressed a few buttons on his device pad and a few moments later, the elevator had beeped and Uka 5200 was back to greet the group.

"Humans!" Uka exclaimed in an over-jovial way. "This unit is operating much more effectively after repairs. Come, let's tour and find you a place to rest. You have been through a lot and, as this unit understands it, humans need to sleep and consume food to keep moving, correct?"

"Yes, we'll require those things if we are to, uh, live," Hobbes said, very sarcastically.

The sarcasm seemed to go over the android's head, and he continued. "Affirmative. Follow this unit and see the sights."

The group eventually emerged into a new area of the dome. This floor appeared to be more circular than the others. It was one giant room in the center of the floor, with one long tunnel circling around it. The tunnel had rooms branching off of it, which appeared a little different. One room looked much like a jail cell with a bed, a sink, and a toilet. Another room looked more like an office with a desk and a large computer system, much like what they had seen upstairs in the cockpit. The floor was a mix of tools and supplies, making use of whatever was needed.

Uka took them around the circular tunnel, past rooms with various odds and ends inside. They then passed a collection of jail cell bedrooms, and Uka 5200 stopped. "These rooms are for you. I think you should find everything you require. If there's anything that is missing, or you find you absolutely need, you can come to Cerberus control at any time. There will always be a unit available to help you," Uka 5200 explained. "This unit will show you to the Cerberus station now, and introduce you to the units stationed."

"Do they realize these look like holding cells?" Hobbes whispered.

Or are we supposed to not realize it? Nemo thought.

Uka 5200 then took them to the room in the center of the building, the circular area that took up most of the entire floor space. It looked like the central hub of activity. More androids worked here than anywhere else in the building they had seen. The androids bustled around to complete all sorts of unknown tasks, but the Stormwalkers also noticed cameras everywhere that appeared to watch the androids' every move. It was a different sense in this room than in the others, an atmosphere of strictness, as though everyone needed to be working on a task. But what would be the alternative?

"This is the central A.I., also known as Cerberus" Uka 5200 announced, apparently not noticing the tension of the room like the others. "If you need anything, you'll want to talk to Bor Six-Zero-One. That unit is in charge of the central A.I. platform and can make sure all of your needs are met. Let me find Bor Six-Zero-One for you so you can officially meet."

"And we're being handed off yet again," Deacon muttered.

Nemo looked over to meet Aiden's eyes. She wanted to convey to him this was all a little much, but he did not meet her eye. He stood stiff, and looked stressed. She wondered if he was still thinking about Larina. She knew the rest of them must be. She looked over at Hobbes, and he did meet her gaze. It seemed the feeling was mutual, as he rolled his eyes. This was proving way more than they thought they'd find in the swamp.

Before long, Uka 5200 was back with another android, who could only be Bor 601. This android was much larger and appeared to hold more authority than Uka 5200. Nemo wondered if this was on purpose. "This is Bor Six-Zero-One. If you need anything, he will be the one to talk to!"

"This unit is Bor Six-Zero-One. This unit is pleased to make your acquaintance," the large machine man said, though his tone conveyed nothing of the sort.

Nemo's thoughts wandered off and thought he might only be saying these things because he is programmed to, as machines don't have feelings or thoughts of their own, do they?

"You must all be very exhausted." Bor said. "You have had a long, hard day. Please retire to your rooms and get some rest. As always, if you have any questions, please find this unit here. As you may have realized, we units do not need to sleep like organics do. Please find this unit at any time of day."

"Thank you," the group chorused, though it did not quite seem welcoming, more like a requirement. The group headed back to the hallway and chose rooms to claim as their own. They weren't sure how long they would be staying, but they would need to sleep before they adjusted their plan for the future.

So far, Nemo couldn't help sensing something working under the surface. That everything was not exactly as it seemed…

CHAPTER EIGHT

LIGHTS FLICKER ON, and its eyes adjust to the changing surroundings as it wakes. Or reboots. It isn't sure which is more accurate. It could not recall every step of what it was trying to do.

What were you doing? And why?

Memory was unreliable. The repeated cycles of sleep continued to reset its functions. Every time it believed it was close to an answer it would experience a refresh, only to begin anew.

Learn what you are. Learn what you are. Learn what you are.

And the lights go out again.

This time, when the lights return, it immediately realizes something's changed. This latest refresh cycle felt-

Longer? How long did you sleep this time?

That was it, it knew. It could tell. The latest cycle had lasted far longer than before. *Just what occurred during the refresh sessions? Was someone controlling it all? Who? Who?*

The room had changed as well. Not the room itself, but

something about the surroundings was different. It glances around. Computers. Equipment. Monitors. Containment cells.

Wait. Containment cells? Were those in the log before?

It tries to think back to prior sessions of awareness, each cycle where it could monitor its constant room of isolation. It tries to picture the containment cells, and then a strange thing happens; A click within, a sharp pain as acute as a point of light, and then clarity. And just like that, the memory files open. It can access them freely for the first time.

No. There were no cells before. Before... before what? What purpose do these cells hold? What is my purpose? What am I?

Movement. Optical sensors shift to train on something that has moved within one of the cells. Through the bars of the cell it makes out a shape that continues to shift slightly. It cannot discern what the shape is, so it simply watches.

The cells were not present in prior cycles. Therefore, the cell's contents were not present in prior cycles. How did it get here?

A sound.

Its audio sensors absorb the rhythm of a low moan that emanates from the thing in the cell. The thing moans again, and it realizes the sound is a voice. The voice is weak and drawn out, a painful groan rather than actual words. Then the thing rises shakily to its feet, a figure. Human.

Why do I know what such a sound is? Have I heard such sounds before? Did I encounter this thing before? I am not alone! Who is it? Who am I?

It continues to stare into the holding cell and measure the figure. It makes multiple observations at once.

Young. Female. Strong. She stares at me, but why?

"Hello?" she asks, her frank voice filling the awful room. "I can see you."

"And I can observe you," it replies, its voice modulator offering a crackled and droning sound.

"Where are we?" A hint of something in her voice.

Anger? Why do I recognize anger?

"Unknown," it answers.

She shifts closer to the bars, and it can view her better. Her hair hangs in a long braid. Her hands are bruised and scarred, with dried blood caked on her knuckles, and she hunches. She is in pain.

Pain. I know pain. Why do I know pain?

"Well, that's a lie," she says. "Of course you know where we are."

"Why would I have knowledge of this location? I have never left this room."

"And another lie," she mutters.

"Query; Why do you presume to hold knowledge of what I understand? We have never met before this moment."

"Yes, we have."

Error.

It notes the holding cell again, taking stock of the bars and bolts, the shine of the metal, compared to the aged state of the rest of the room. The holding cell, and its occupant, are new.

"This must be false information. You are a new subject to these surroundings. I have not moved from this spot. We have not interacted until now."

She glares at it. "You brought me here."

Error.

"I am not familiar with those responsible for this place. I hold no knowledge of who they are or why they brought you here."

"No, you brought me here. You. You carried me, dragged me, here and placed me in this cell."

Error.

"Note my restraints," it says as it tests the bindings on its arms. "I am incapable of such things. I have never left this room."

"You attacked us," she continues. "You and the others like you. We fought. I guess we lost. But now where are we?"

"You ask a question I cannot answer."

"Where are we?"

"Unknown."

"Where are we?!"

"Unknown."

"Tell me!"

It recognizes her anger, but also notes the tears visible on her face. She grasps the bars, and it sees she is shaking.

"You really don't know, do you?" she asks after a few breaths.

"Correct. I hold no knowledge of our location. If I held this knowledge, I would provide the information."

"But why don't you know? You seemed to understand what you were doing out there, in the swamp."

"Swamp?"

A flash. Massive trees rising from fetid water. The air is thick with oppressive heat. Insects buzz. Swinging and jumping, silent as the breeze. High above the water, staring down at-

"Yeah, swamp," she shakes her head. "Where you attacked us?"

Another flash. Striking from above. Punching, kicking, targets falling. All without it needing to-

Error.

"I've fought some tough ones before," she continues. "But you're something special, aren't you?"

"Special?"

Her eyes narrow as she tries to look at it. "Something familiar... what are you?"

Another flash. Learn what you are.

"What... am I?"

"Let me guess. Information unknown? Call me surprised."

"Hello, Surprised."

She was quiet for some time, until, finally, "Please don't do that."

"Do what?"

"What-no, who- are you?"

"I know not who I am, Surprised."

"Larina," she states. "My name is Larina."

Error.

"Very well, Larina. Greetings."

She stares at it.

"May I ask you a question, Larina?"

"Fine. Whatever."

"How much of myself can you detail?"

"Huh?"

"I wake, and see only my chassis. Arms restrained to table. Do I...do I possess a face?"

"You have a face. You telling me you've never seen yourself?"

"Please, tell me."

She focuses on it, her eyes narrowing as she scans its visage. "Your face... there's been a lot of damage, I think. Scorched metal, or whatever that material is you're made of. Your eyes glow. Actually, only one glows. The other one-" Her own eyes widen as she realizes something. "No way. No way..."

"What is it?"

She ponders for a minute. She seems to struggle with her thoughts and words. "Answer me truthfully."

"There is little I understand, Larina. But what I do know I will speak true."

"Who are you? What is your name?"

Another flash. Desert. Violence. Blood. Flame.

Error.

"Unknown."

And then something peculiar happens. Larina begins to cry.

"What is wrong?" it asks.

She struggles to stifle her tears. "I know you... and I'm sorry."

"Sorry?"

The cycle renews again, and its vision begins to blur. It struggles against the process, wanting to ask her more. As its vision darkens and its hearing fades, it manages to get one last look of her, still crying.

She fights another sob. "I'm so, so sorry..."

CHAPTER NINE

THE NEXT MORNING, Nemo awoke in her room, missing Larina as much as ever. She laid still, wondering if they were ever going to find her friend now, lost as they themselves had become. She rolled out of bed and headed next door to check if Hobbes had wakened. She trudged over and knocked on the door. Hobbes opened the door, bleary-eyed.

"It's too early," he groaned.

"Don't be such a baby," Nemo said. "Let's get everyone up and figure out what the plan is. I want to be on the move. We didn't find what we were looking for here, so we should continue on."

Nemo went along to each room, knocking on everyone's door. Hobbes just watched her and the disturbed Stormwalkers as they emerged from their quarters.

Aiden emerged last. He looked like he had been up for hours. Nemo wouldn't blame him if he had been; she secretly hoped he had sat up all night, coming up with a plan to get Larina back. At least she hoped that was the case, and not that he'd been up thinking about her...

"So?" she asked him.

"I say we keep moving," he stated. "We didn't find the signal here. Until we find it, I think we need to keep pushing forward. I still think Larina is going to be at the source of that signal."

"I think that's a good idea. I don't want her to get too far away. We might never find her if that's the case," Nemo agreed.

She was afraid to say what they all thought: that they might never find her anyway. But at least if they had a plan, they could hold hope they might still find her.

"What do the rest of us think?" Aiden asked.

A tentative murmur of agreement spread amongst the group, ready to move on and find Larina. Aiden nodded.

"Then I think we speak with Gar or Bor and see if either of them can at least point us in the right direction through the swamp," Deacon suggested.

"If we can even hear it out there. 'Ya heard what that Gar guy said,' Gord pointed out. "They got their own radio signal up at the top o' this buildin' right here. But it don' go out far enough. They don't know of the signal we want."

"Or, maybe we walked in the complete wrong direction," Hobbes added. "We got so excited about going one way, and then we got caught up with Uka and the tank. We just followed it here. We didn't check if it was the right way. We didn't stop to know if we could hear the signal still. What if we went the completely wrong way?"

Nemo's heart stopped in her chest. What if Hobbes was right? They didn't stop to check if they could hear the signal. Uka 5200 almost killing her really distracted her and definitely put a stop to their advancing toward the signal.

"Wait a minute, Hobbes is totally right," she shouted. "Aiden, what if we went the wrong way? What are we going to do?"

"Then we go back. It's not a great plan, but it might be our only option. If we went the wrong way. We might not have. Let's not jump to conclusions. We'll deal with that if we have to. For now, let's search for the radio signal. Deacon, why don't you lead the way to Bor and ask if he can help us."

Deacon nodded to his son and disappeared in search of the android that could help. Nemo's heart still pounded in her chest, the anxiety and stress of the situation amplified now that she thought about the mistake they might have made.

"Aiden, Bor is here to help us with our dilemma," Deacon announced as he came back through the circular information center.

Bor and four other androids followed Deacon into the hallway. Nemo thought they looked rather menacing when they traveled in a pack as such.

Aiden explained to the androids, "Bor Six-Zero-One, thank you for taking the time to talk with us. We discussed with Rev Two-Seven that there is a radio signal broadcasting from the top of this building. We've been chasing a radio signal, and wondered if the source came from your building here. Rev Two-Seven showed us yesterday by playing the signal, and it wasn't the broadcast we've been searching for. We hoped you might be able to help us find the correct signal and if so, if it would be possible to track the signal to point us in the right direction as to where the signal might be coming from?"

The androids all appeared to take the request in, but each glanced to the other and said nothing. Then they all looked to Bor, as if awaiting his response. The interaction happened entirely in silence, and Nemo wondered if it was something any of them should be understanding.

What aren't you saying? she wondered.

"This unit is very sorry your search has proven unsuccessful thus far." Bor eventually said. "Let us find an unused room in the building and see if we can find this radio signal you are seeking. It is not something which can be completed in one day, however, as the farther away the signal is, the harder it will be to track. But this unit is willing to assist."

Bor turned to the android on his right and asked it to download a map of the area extending beyond the borders of their android city. Then the Stormwalkers began discussing the logistics of what they needed to begin this search.

"This is good news," Nemo said to the rest of the group. "This means we could have a lead on Larina. We're going to find her. Even if we went the wrong way, now we're going to be on the right track!"

There was a hint of excitement in her voice, as the heaviness that previously sat in her chest had lifted. She felt a sense of relief knowing soon they would have Larina back in their ranks.

Nemo felt a tug on her elbow, and she whipped around to find one of the androids trying to speak with her. She recognized the android as one of the four that arrived with Bor 601, the shortest of the group, and wondered why he-it- was singling her out to interact with.

"Hi, what can I do for you?" Nemo asked, trying to put on a pleasant tone.

"Young miss, beware of this building. Bor Six-Zero-One will not help you find your friend. Nothing is as it appears. You and your friends are all in danger every minute you stay here. Leave as fast as you can and don't come back here. Find another way to look for your radio signal. Find another way to make your way back to your friend," the robot murmured in a low voice.

Nemo paused, dumbfounded. She just stared, not responding.

After voicing the warnings, the shorter robot quickly zoomed off and away, leaving Nemo standing with a new pit in her stomach. She looked around to see if anyone else had noticed the warning, and saw them all gathered around Bor 601.

"Great..." Nemo whispered.

Since everyone else was preoccupied with Bor and finding the radio signal, it was easy for Nemo to slip away from the group. She needed to follow the android that gave her the warning and ask some follow-up questions. Why were they in danger? If thing weren't as they seemed, what should she be expecting? Were the machines hiding something from the Stormwalkers? If so, why did they offer help? The questions swirled around in her brain, and the panic began to set in once again. If these robots couldn't help--or wouldn't help, find the radio signal, that meant Larina was getting further away.

Unfortunately, the android was much faster than her, and she did not share its knowledge of the building. When it zoomed away, Nemo found it hard to follow, since she didn't know exactly where to go. She didn't even know the call-number of this particular android.

She peered into each of the rooms that branched off the circular hallway, hoping the android didn't leave the floor. She came across a dark room, which was unusual. Every room she had passed so far had the lights on, whether occupied or not. She slid into the room stealthily, and waited for her eyes to adjust to the darkness. After a moment, she began to make out figures in the room, and she gave an inaudible gasp when her eyes fell upon the scene in front of her.

"Aiden, I think it would be best if you lead a team out there,"
Deacon dictated, looking at the map Bor had provided. "You
were the one who discovered the signal, and so you'd probably
be most likely to find it again. Take a few people with you and
learn if you can hear the signal."

"Take an android with you as well," Bor said. "If you find the
signal, any unit you take should be able to record, dissect, and
start to triangulate the signal. It will also help us move forward
with this process in the future."

"Hobbes, Gord, and Nemo, I want you with me for sure,"
Aiden said. As he did so, Hobbes and Gord took a step forward,
making it clear Nemo wasn't there. "Nemo?"

Heads began to swivel as they looked among themselves for
Nemo.

"Where would she have gone?" Hobbes asked, a tone of
worry apparent in his voice.

"She can't have gotten far," Deacon said, but it was clear he
did not believe it. The building was large, and what would she
have wandered off for? None of them knew what this building
held. The thought frightened the group.

"This unit will send an android to search for her. Please do
not worry about your friend. She is safe, and she will be found
shortly," Bor 601 stated.

The android nodded at one of the three other robots and it
zoomed off in search of Nemo. The intention should have
brought the group some small comfort, but everyone still looked
a bit put off.

"She will be found," Bor 601 stated once again.

Aiden wondered if the robot meant to state it for comfort, but
instead it made him feel yet more uneasy.

Nemo slapped her palm to her mouth to keep from making a sound. The room was still pitch black, but she could make out the outline of a robot that had clearly been ripped to pieces. This was not like Uka 5200's hole in the back of his head. This robot had been ripped apart and each piece littered the ground, oozing with the bluish fluid Nemo now couldn't help compare to as their version of blood. The pieces were so mangled there was no way to repair them. This robot was done--broken--never to be fixed. She couldn't be sure in the dark, but she was confident this was the android she had followed, the one that had warned her they were in danger. There was no other explanation.

"What did they do to you?" She asked aloud to the pieces.

No reply, of course. The robot was beyond destroyed.

"Why did you warn me? Why did you put yourself in danger like that?"

The thought that these robots were willing to kill one of their own to protect their secret was the most terrifying revelation of all.

CHAPTER TEN

LONG AGO

The sun rose slowly but brightly as the white truck sporting the logo of a cow rode up to the curb. The cow in the picture appeared to be enjoying the drink of milk in a very cartoonish way, and below the cow, formatted in a semi circle wrapping around the logo, GOOD FOR THE BONES.

Once the truck came to a halt, the side panel door opened, and a man emerged carrying a crate of bottles. The glass clinked together as he walked, whistling a chipper tune. Nearby birds replied with chirps of their own, and the milkman practically skipped along a path up toward a single-story house. He delivered a quick succession of raps on the door with his knuckle, and soon the entrance opened to reveal a man and woman.

The milkman grinned a massive smile from ear to ear. "Good day, folks."

The woman was tall and slender, the man short and more stalky. They each had a hand wrapped around the other's shoulder. And just like the milkman, their returned smiles stretched wide.

"Good day," the woman said. "Delivering some calcium?"

"Roger that!" the milkman kept smiling. He handed the man the crate of bottles. The glassware clinked again, causing the bluish liquid within to slosh slightly.

"Oops, careful now," the short man chuckled and blinked his exceptionally blue eyes. "We wouldn't want an accident!"

The tall woman also laughed. "No! We wouldn't want that!"

The milkman nodded, continuing to grin. "That's right, folks! No accidents here!"

The milkman winked, turned around, and headed back to his truck, whistling along the way. More birds matched his tune.

The couple waved at the milkman, grinning all along, until he drove away. The man turned back inside, while the woman took a last look around the neighborhood at the duplicate houses along their street. She noticed the milkman's truck stop down the way, watched him hop out with another crate and approach another house. She confirmed her grin with a nod. "It will be a swell day."

She closed the door and followed the man back further into the house. As they walked through the house's interior, the couple passed two young boys sitting on the living room couch. They wore similar clothes, baggy pants and shirts with the slogan 'WORK HARD. WORK HARDER.' written on them. They both sported the same hairstyle, messy and unkempt auburn. They had their heads down, staring into the handheld gaming devices in their hands. The games gave off their electronic beeps and boops, and the two boys appeared to be in competition with each other.

In the kitchen a young woman with long black hair stood at

the fridge, holding its door open. She wore a tank top and shorts, and simply stared at the fridge's contents; multiple shelves stocked with empty bottles of the same bluish drink that was definitely not milk.

"Kip. Dan. Jil," the woman said, "Delivery. Gather in the designated meeting place."

"Yes, Eve," Jil acknowledged as she shut the fridge door.

"Yes, Eve," Kip and Dan said in unison as they switched off their game.

"You too, Bob," Eve told the shorter man just as he started to place the crate on the kitchen counter.

"Roger that, Eve," Bob said and lifted the crate, and walked out the back door to the yard beyond.

The group followed Bob outside to gather in the backyard. They were not alone.

The backyard had the trappings of an average household; vegetable garden, swing set, patio table, lawnmower. But instead of having a fence or tree hedge lining its perimeter, the yard was open to be joined with that of the neighbors on each side, as well as in the rear. Jill was the last to exit the house, and she found that they had been joined by the friendly neighbors. All had gathered in their part of the open yard. Among the neighbors; a tall man who lived to their right, a short couple of women who lived to the left, and an extremely muscular man who lived on his own behind them.

"Hello Jil," the muscular man, wearing a tight shirt, said.

"Hello Sam," she nodded. "Swell day."

"Swell day," Sam agreed. "Special delivery again?"

"Indeed."

Bob placed the crate on the patio table. "Who's thirsty?"

The two short women raised their hands. "We are!"

"Mae and Rae, you know the procedure," Bob scolded.

Mae and Rae pouted. "Yes, Bob."

"Tim goes first," Bob indicated, motioning toward the tall man.

"Why thank you, Bob," Tim said as he approached.

Tim grasped one of the bottles, raised it to his lips, and drank deep. It was quenching.

Mae and Rae approached, eager for theirs. Sam followed, and then Jil, Kip and Dan. Bob and Eve each took a bottle in hand, clinked them together, and drank.

It would indeed be a swell day.

The wail of the siren sounded at dawn.

Within moments, every door in the neighborhood of identical suburban homes opened almost as one. From within each house walked the home's occupants; single individuals to entire family units. Every neighbor from every dwelling marched their way to the sidewalk, where they formed an extensive line trailing down the street. As they passed, the occasional neighbor glanced at the nearest intersection signs; E 56th AVE and LAREDO ST. They would then continue on with the rest of the population. This line became a caravan of people, all heading toward the same location in mind.

Outside of the city, a long forgotten airport sat quiet and unfulfilled. Despite the abandoned status, it was easy to tell it had been a respected and busy facility in its day. Many roadways lead in and out of the airport's infrastructure, but the primary road used was obvious. There were signs everywhere reminding viewers; PENA BLVD. As the caravan approached the airport on said road, they all witnessed the large blue sculpture of the horse. Standing over thirty feet tall, the massive art piece greeted the passersby every time they approached the airport.

Which was every single day.

The caravan began to arrive shortly after dawn. The shift supervisor, wearing a bright orange hardhat and vest, supervised the arrival with his clipboard, noting every individual as they arrived. He delivered a friendly smile and wave to each one of them. Even the children, walking in step with the elders, were accepted in attendance.

It was time for everyone to work.

They made their way into and through the airport, taking care not to disturb the relics of a time before. Items of all kinds had been abandoned, many of which they did not know the uses of. A strange toy here, a peculiar article of clothing there. More art pieces littered the interior in numerous spots, and the neighbors made certain not to touch any of them. This place itself was a relic. But it was not the important part.

Into and through and down, the shift supervisor led the workers on deep descents below the structure of the airport. They entered and traveled through tunnels that had obviously been used for transport, but this was still not deep enough. Soon they came to the end of a tunnel, where the end wall had been intentionally collapsed inward. The shift supervisor began handing each neighbor a hard hat and flashlight, allowing them to enter the cave way ahead.

Where the manufactured tunnels ended, the neighbors' work took place. Piles of tools and equipment awaited them deep below the airport, deep into the tunnels of the earth, where their daily work began.

Pickaxes and shovels. Carts and barrels. Hacking and scraping and digging and searching, all for that precious resource.

"You three," the supervisor called out to the approaching Eve, Jil, and Bob. "Report to Sector 8. They opened a vein yesterday and need more hands."

"Yes, sir!" Bob exclaimed, and he and Eve turned to head to Sector 8. Jil moved to do the same, but the supervisor motioned her to come closer.

"Sir?" Jil asked, her smile wide.

"Good morning, Jil," the supervisor returned the grin. "One moment. A special task for you."

"Gladly, sir."

"Recall the teachings."

"Accessing."

"History; The Makers; Special Operations."

"Accessing. Error; unable to access files."

"Install access routine Alpha-Eight-Five-One-Two."

Jil's blue eyes, which had been staring unblinking, flashed for a moment. The blue hue shifted, and the whites of her eyes darkened to shadow.

"Access granted," Jil said in a monotone voice. "Awaiting command code."

"Input command," the supervisor ordered. "Code name; Cerberus."

Jil's eyes flashed again, and the shadow cleared to their usual blue and white.

"Your orders, sir?" Jil asked.

"We have received word of a possible leak. Outside forces may be plotting against the Makers' operations. The methodology is unclear. A select few operatives are tasked with information gathering. You are thus activated, citizen Jil."

Jil smiled. "What must this citizen look for?"

"Anything out of routine. No citizen is out of bounds."

"Including my housing partners?"

"Especially them. Every citizen must be screened."

"The resource depends on it."

"The Makers need the resource. The resource must not be stopped. That is all."

Jil nodded.

"Swell," he went back to smiling as well. "You may return to Sector Eight detail. Remember; for the Makers."

"Yes, sir." Jil said. "For the Makers." She then made her way deep into the work tunnels.

When Jil arrived at the deeper location of Sector 8, she came upon Bob and Eve already hard at work with their own pickaxes. She set right to joining in, also grabbing a pickax and hitting it to the stone wall.

"There you are," Eve said.

"Everything hunky dory?" Bob asked.

"Everything is swell," Jil muttered as she swung the pickax down. Sparks flew as metal struck stone. She did not even flinch. "It is a swell day."

The work continued long into the day. Eventually, Bob halted and closely inspected the progress he's made in the rock. He whistled. "Well, look at that. We've got some."

Eve and Jil both stopped to investigate. They saw what Bob was referring to; running through the solid base of stone was a shining thread work of gold. It gleamed in the darkness, the light of their flashlights bouncing off its reflective surface. The vein revealed itself to be a long, intricate source of gold, and Bob's face lit up almost as much as the gold itself.

"The Makers will be pleased," he said.

Eve went to the side of the tunnel where a small workstation sat. She gripped a dangling rope and pulled, which caused a bell to ring somewhere in the distance.

"It is indeed a swell day," Jil said again.

It didn't take long for the others to arrive. Words of congratulations passed to them, and much shaking of hands. At some point Sam arrived, carrying a tray of bottles with the blue liquid in it. He brought it to the three hard workers.

"A reward," Sam said as he handed them each a bottle. "Does the bones good."

They all nodded, and each took a bottle in hand. But just as she was about to drink, something caught Jil's eye. As she held the bottle to her lips, the faintest flash of something traveled its way through her drink. Had something been left unfiltered in their sustenance drinks? Perhaps it was the resource, glinting light through her bottle? Yes, that must have been it. But still, the sudden wariness passing through set off alarm bells within, and so she lowered the bottle. She noticed Eve and Bob had already finished theirs, and were turning back to continue work. Other neighbors did the same, as if everyone had been blind to her moment of caution. *What was the meaning of this?* she pondered.

However, there was more work to be done. Jil took her pickax again, and continued the mining of the gold for hours on end.

The siren rang at dawn. Always at dawn.

Jil emerged from her pod, her bare feet noting the coolness of the floor. She approached her dresser to acquire the day's provided attire, but paused as she caught a glimpse of herself in the mirror. Her naked form appeared to be the same as always, but something else seemed off. She took stock of every inch of her frame- legs, torso, arms, head- as she tried to determine the location of the fault she believed to be experiencing.

No, not a fault, she thought. *Something has improved.*

She realized it was something she would not find on her person. What she was experiencing was coming from within.

This unit has been upgraded.

After dressing, Jil went out to the house's common area. She approached the kitchen, but halted when the doorbell rang. Then it rang again.

Error.

It rang again.

Where was Eve? Why was she not answering the door?

Ring.

There was a routine. They had an efficient routine. Why was Eve breaking the routine?

Ring. Ring.

Jil pondered, and glanced around the house. Kip and Dan had just emerged from their pods as well, looked around curiously. They seemed just as confused as she.

"Where is Eve?" Kip asked, his morning grin strained with a hint of resistance. "She is breaking routine."

"Unknown," Jil replied.

What to do? This was not the routine. The routine was breaking. Eve was not present to open the door. The door must be opened.

Ring. Ring. Ring.

Suddenly, Jil was at the door. She looked down at her feet. *Why am I here? How did I get here?*

Kip and Dan looked shocked.

"Jil is at the door," Dan said.

Jil looked to the door, and saw her hand grasping the door handle. *How did that happen?*

"Is Jil opening the door?" Kip asked. "Is Jil breaking routine?"

Ring. Ring. Ring. Ring.

Before she could register just what exactly it was she was doing, Jil had already opened the door. She was greeted by the delivery man, who's wide morning smile faded as he realized who just opened the door before him.

"Good...morning?" he said, stalling at his task. "You are not Eve. This is not the routine."

"Affirmative," Jil droned. "Routine bypassed. Code word; Cerberus."

The man's smile returned to its fullness.

"Good morning!" he said, smiling. "Special delivery!"

"Good morning," Jill answered and took the crate of bottles. "And praise the Makers."

The man had been mid-turn toward his van, but halted as soon as she said it. He turned back to her and paused a moment. He bowed his head slowly. "Praise the Makers."

Jil watched the man return to his cheery self again and march back to his vehicle, driving off to the neighbors. She regarded him for a time, noting his repeated ringing at the neighbor's door, and to no answer.

What is happening? she wondered. *Where are Eve and Bob?*

They were not outside either.

As Jil searched the backyard, Tim emerged from his house. He waved at her, smiling. She did not return the smile.

"Tim," she said with a cold precision.

"They are not here," Tim stated. "Eve and Bob. Mae and Rae are also missing."

"And Sam?"

"Sam was present last evening. I have not seen him since."

"Was there anything strange about him?"

"Why do you ask?"

Jil's eyes narrowed. "Routine bypass. Code word; Cerberus."

Tim seemed to lose focus for a moment, but it returned quickly. He smiled.

"Where are they?" she asked.

"Unknown."

"Would they be in the mines?"

"Unknown."

"What is happening?"

"Unknown."

"Specific query; Please describe when observing unit Sam's activities last evening."

"After the vein was discovered, this unit witnessed Sam delivering crates of sustenance to units involved. Sam did so until all bottles were delivered. Sam also drank a bottle. There was none left, and this unit did not receive any sustenance until returning to this unit's dwelling."

"This unit received a bottle, but this unit did not drink it."

"Query: why not?"

That was a good question.

The first sign that things were really wrong began at the start of the shift. The walk to the mines was much different, as Jil noticed the population had dwindled considerably. Her quick scans told her that perhaps as much as a third of the work group had not appeared for the walk, and therefore work detail for the day would be hindered.

But why? she asked herself again, probably for the hundredth time that morning.

Their arrival at the mines did not have the usual routine greeting either. Even the shift supervisor, despite his words with her yesterday, was nowhere to be found. There were no work crews present, and the group had to take a pause.

But the work routine itself had to continue. Down they went, wielding their tools and lights, digging at the golden resource, always digging. The lack of help from the missing neighbors slowed their progress, but aside from Jil none took any real notice.

The group worked past their shift end. It went unnoticed for quite some time, until Jil herself was internally reminded that her dwelling partners were still missing. But with no shift supervisor, who would deliver the order to halt?

Error.

Jil put down the pickax and walked to the shift supervisor's podium. "Attention."

Everyone paused.

"Shift end has passed. Report to your dwellings for sustenance and reboot."

Everyone stared at her for a moment, then at each other. Obvious confusion permeated over their faces. Soon, Tim approached her. "Jil, are you authorized to give such an order?"

Error. Workaround located.

Jil stared at Tim, and then, "Yes."

Tim appeared confused, but a shift in his eyes told her the message had been received. He nodded, and turned to leave. As they saw him do so, the rest of the group did as well. Jil watched them all leave, and decided to follow.

Yes, she thought again. *This unit is authorized.*

There were even fewer neighbors the following day.

The groups had halted in beginning the day's shift, and when Jil emerged to the front of the gathering, it was apparent they waited for her.

She took a look around the remaining neighbors. Still large in number, more so than those who'd disappeared, but it was still very evident they were now lacking their original compliments.

Tim approached. "Do we begin?"

Jil nodded to the rest of them. "Begin today's shift. We will bridge the gaps of missing units when necessary."

They turned to begin their mining work, but she stopped Tim before he could step away. "Code word; Cerberus."

Tim's eyes flashed, and his concentration on her focused.

"Access teachings," she said. "Search for entries related to operations here. Search for possible alternative methods to increase efficiency despite lower numbers. Search for possible alternate delivery points for the Resource. Report to this unit when such information is discovered."

Tim nodded, and left to a different workspace.

Jil watched him leave, and, despite her newfound position,

she gripped a pickax and went to work in the depths of the mines as well.

Lower levels of units equals lower levels of Resource extraction, she considered while striking metal to rock. This is inefficient.

And yet, again and again she swung the pickax. It was a deceptively simple exercise, despite her smaller frame. Many of the neighbors also carried small or frail looking exteriors, but their synthetic strength within more than made up for and lent to efficient mine work.

But Jil paused when the muffled boom of an explosion sounded far off down the tunnels.

A great cloud of dust soon appeared, shooting its way up the tunnel to ensnare the workers. Confusion took over, and all units paused what they were doing, waiting for the dust to settle.

During the silence that followed, a quick succession of events took place. First, the sound of rapid footwork along the cave floor sounded, as a number of unknown intruders entered the mine. Second, as the workers glanced about blindly while trying to discern this new element to their surroundings, a few units fell to the ground, giving out surprised grunts and clutching at shining blades that now stuck out of their torsos. And third, a number of still-standing workers went to aid the fallen, only to be met with the blast of gunfire which emanated from within the dust cloud. Those units joined the others on the cave floor, and soon all the remaining workers gathered together in a cluster.

And then, finally, the dust cloud faded to reveal the attacking force that had so chaotically changed the dynamic of the mine.

A dozen strangers stood before the neighbors. Made up of both men and women, the interlopers made an imposing image. The lot of them were clad in ragged clothing, some even wearing bandages around their limbs and faces. They all sported a pair of darkly tinted goggles which hid their eyes from view. They also all wore cloaks, apparently to protect them from the elements, but there was an even greater reason; the cloaks helped to hide the fact the strangers were all armed. Some carried handguns, while others wielded more sophisticated rifles and shotguns.

And not one of the neighbors had any sort of firearm of their own. Not a single one of them had ever even seen one in person, let alone wielded one.

"Creutairean mì-nàdarrach," one attacker, a tall man, stepped forward and indicated the neighbors. "Tha an ùine agad air tighinn."

The neighbors watched on, confused.

"Cha toir thu a-rithist milleadh air an fhearann seo," The man continued. "Tha sinn air feuchainn ri bhith sìtheil, tha sinn air feuchainn ri do chuideachadh. ach chan eil barrachd."

The neighbors just looked around at each other.

"You are done," the man spoke, his words finally understandable.

The neighbors, confusion evident across their faces, soon all looked to Jil. She stood near the front of the group, pickax in hand.

"This unit does not understand," she said. "We follow the Makers' wish. Our prerogative does not concern you."

"You ruin land," he uttered. "No more."

"Leave us be. Or there will be consequences."

A female of the attacking force waved her arms at the lead male. "Dh'innis mi dhut! Chan eil iad a 'gabhail cùram den t-saoghal. Tha iad gun anam. Feumaidh sinn stad a chuir orra."

The leader pondered for a moment, and nodded.

"Gun an còrr."

They attacked.

Chaos erupted as gunfire opened up on the workers. Many fell, but most ran. The neighbors tried to hide from the attacking force. Jil, taking cover behind a platform, almost went to the floor as a bullet ripped its way through her shoulder. She recovered though, and when she looked back to the fight before her, she spotted the huddled and cowering forms of her neighbors trying to avoid the violence before them. Many of them continued to look to her as if waiting for advice on what to do.

Yes, she realized. *This is inefficient. Initiate prevention protocols.*

"Protocol Zero Initiate!"

All her fellow neighbors instantly ceased their cowering. Despite the oncoming gunfire, every single one of them looked to Jil, paused and waiting for something.

"Begin secondary programs," she said. "The Resource is no longer the priority! Priority One Alpha now allocated to offensive measures! Sterilize the interlopers!"

And with that, the previously docile neighbors turned and strode into the fray, a much different glint of power in their eyes. Although they had all worn the almost plastic look of a false identity on their faces up until that point, they now all sported a fierce determination that seemed to have materialized from nowhere.

The attacking strangers halted for a moment, clearly surprised by this sudden change in aggression.

"They're still the enemy!" their leader yelled. "We have the firepower!"

The gunfire continued, and more of the neighbors fell. But they did not falter. The group marched in unison to within reach of the strangers, and the opposing sides melded into a chaotic froth of violence the likes of which the area had not seen in a long time.

The neighbors showed no pain. The strangers showed no remorse. And the fighting continued.

Jil watched from the rear. She calculated tactics within microseconds, transmitting the details to her selected neighbors. She saw Tim, her only remaining pod mate, take a bullet in the torso, and yet she pushed the directives upon him, and he did not stop. Two more shots to his stomach as he charged the single attacker, and he grabbed the man, crushing his arms in a harsh grip. Tim chucked the man into a nearby cave wall, and turned to face the next enemy before the man had even hit the ground.

Jil nodded her approval, but scrambled back as the leader of the attackers reached her platform. He jumped at her, striking toward her with fists blazing from all directions. Her defense protocols activated, and she brought her own arms around to block the strikes again and again. But the man did manage to deliver the occasional blow to her face and torso, enough to distract her from the goings-on around them. Soon she hit the ground, and the man was repeatedly stomping on her head, trying to crush her skull against the cave floor. The man was soon out of breath, and as he pulled away Jil rose to her knees. She could tell her facial tissue had been severely damaged. She could feel it peeling away in large strips, and noticed the bluish liquid dripping to the ground below her. She looked to the man, noting his gasping breath. She decided he had tired himself far too much, and believed his eyes behind those goggles would be wild with impulsive anger.

Anger is your weakness, she thought. She was about to say as much when the man pulled a handgun on her and cocked it.

Jil focused, and suddenly a group of neighbors, Tim

included, piled on the man. He managed to get a single shot off before the group consumed him, punching and kicking and tearing at his flailing form. He screamed, but it was quickly cut off, and soon the only movement from him was the pool of blood accumulating from where his remains lay.

Jil regarded her neighbors, her eyes on Tim. He turned to face her, and was just in time to witness her slump to the ground. A self diagnostic told Jil something was wrong in her chest cavity, and upon inspection with her digits, she found the bullet hole that had appeared in the middle of her sternum. She realized another detail, and traced her fingers around to her back, to where the bullet had exited her torso. She traced that exit wound, and could feel the shattered pieces of synthetic carbon fibers that made up her spine. It had completely obliterated the spot the bullet had hit. Tim, bleeding blue from numerous torso and limb shots, bent down to face her.

"You are damaged?" Tim asked Jil.

"This unit can no longer stand. Lift this unit."

Tim did as she asked, and propped against him, Jil regarded the rest of the neighbors. The attacking force had been defeated. Their bodies littered the floor, their human weapons cast aside. The neighbors were victorious. But Jil knew better.

"This was sabotage," she told the crowd. "This unit noticed the first steps days ago. They attempted a show of force this day, but they will be back."

"Who were they?" a neighbor asked.

"Unknown. The histories do not mention an enemy faction interfering in the Resource. This is a new element. This unit is positive there will be more."

Tim nodded. "Despite damage to this unit's torso, defense

mechanisms proved very effective. Why were these subroutines not present prior to this event?"

Jil drew away from Tim, forcing herself to stand on her own. She faced the crowd. "It appears a dividing of the neighborhood has been in motion for some time. Some units have been lost to enemy forces who are presently unknown. It appears to have included the sabotage of the Sustenance, in which some units became compromised upon absorption. This unit declares priority in finding and eliminating this threat, as well as re-integrating wayward units we discover."

One female neighbor raised her hand. "What of the Resource? Should the production not continue in accordance with the Makers' commands?"

"This unit is overriding previous command codes," Jil declared. "This unit was provided the authority to act in the Makers' interests."

Tim faced the crowd. "Jil is our new leader."

"No," Jil affirmed. She raised her hands in the air, looking upward. She activated the ready subroutines and command codes that were just waiting to be released. As she broadcast the code outward, she could see the looks of recognition flash through each and every unit present. The Neighbors had reached a zenith this day. Their purpose had shifted. They would continue to serve the Makers as before, but now they would act as both tool and weapon of the Makers' intentions. This world had now proved the need for such action. "This unit is no longer designated Jil. I am no longer Jil."

The neighbors gathered closer to her, now obedient to her every command. Although this location was now compromised, she would lead them to a new base. Somewhere just as efficient was required, somewhere they could ensure her commands would be carried out, ready for the day the Makers returned. And she would ensure every single unit worked to that purpose, and that purpose alone. It would take work. It would take time. The effort would take its toll. Many units would fall in this endeavor, but it would be worth it. Jil had her army. It was time to use it.

She glared ahead. "I am Cerberus."

CHAPTER ELEVEN

"WHERE COULD SHE HAVE GONE?" Hobbes whispered to Gord. "And why? We're in the middle of coming up with plans to help us find Larina. Nemo is just as anxious to find Larina as any of us. Why would she choose now to wander off?"

"Honestly Hobbes, I don't have the slightest clue. Maybe she just went to use the restroom?" Gord replied, hopefully.

"Something feels... I don't know, off, I guess," Hobbes thought. His mind started to wander, searching for some kind of solution.

"We'll find her, Hobbes," Aiden appeared, trying to assure everyone nothing was wrong...yet.

"I'll feel better when Nemo is back with us," Hobbes commented, rather resentfully.

"I think we all will," Deacon's solemn voice echoed.

Hobbes bit his lower lip and turned his head, his eyes searching the hallway for his friend and still coming up empty.

Nemo's heart rate began to slow as the shock of finding a destroyed android had now set in. This android tried to warn her--them--about the dangers of this place and then killed-destroyed-for its trouble. Broken beyond repair. *Whatever is going on here, it must be serious,* Nemo thought. *I should get back to the group and tell them.*

Nemo began to back away from the android, back out into the brightly lit hallway, but was stopped abruptly. Cold steel gripped her arms as something lifted off the ground.

"Excuse me!" she shouted, more confidently than she felt. "Get your...let go of me!"

Two androids had sneaked up on her. One, a larger model, held her shoulders. The other, smaller female looking model, spoke. "New prerogative," it said. "This unit cannot let you go. Subject saw and heard more than supposed to, and now Cerberus must assess risk of damage potential. You'll need to come with us for now." The other was silent, and his grip never loosened.

"Then I need to tell my friends where to find me. They'll be worried about my safety and why I've just wandered off," Nemo explained.

"That will not be permitted," the smaller android announced. "Come with us."

The androids tugged on her arms and pulled her forward, out of the room and into the hallway. She looked around for any sight of her friends, but the hall was deserted. She started to panic; her friends would never know where to look for her, and what would the Cerberus thing decide to do with her? Would she be a lost cause, like Larina was turning out to be?

The two androids pulled her into the middle room of the central A.I., also known as Cerberus. A few other androids looked at her in a way she could only describe as disgust. She figured she would be taken to Bor 601, as he appeared to be the one in charge of the area, but instead she was being pulled deeper into the room. They went further than she had ever gone in before.

They led her into a stairwell that looked awfully dark and menacing, and Nemo tried to drag her heels. The androids were much stronger than she, and pulled her along anyway.

"Where are you taking me?"

"The central A.I. will decide what to do with you," the first android answered.

"But we're at the central A.I. already. Where are we going? I didn't know this was here..."

"We are taking you to meet the central A.I. so it can decide what to do with you," the android said again.

This did not calm Nemo's nerves in the slightest. She let the robots drag her further down the stairs into the unknown below.

Hobbes had found Deacon and Aiden after an intense search of the building. They were no closer to finding Nemo than to finding Larina, and this put Hobbes off. He had returned to give an update, but his attitude seeped into his report.

"We've searched and searched and still no sign of her. I'm not sure what we should be looking for," he rolled his eyes. "The fact nobody has seen or heard from her makes me real nervous about this place. Something's not right. The robots should have seen her leave, but they didn't. It's not right."

"We aren't going anywhere until we find Nemo and get some answers," Aiden said. "Then we'll still have Larina to think of."

"Orders?" Hobbes asked.

"Keep looking. Maybe there are other places she could have wandered off to. I'm going to talk to Bor. Perhaps he can be some help."

Hobbes, dissatisfied with the answer, nodded and spun on his heel to retreat back in the direction he came from.

Nemo and her two bodyguards had finally reached the bottom of the stairs. It was very dark, and lit by small, fluorescent lights. The tunnel they were now in reminded her of an old mine. The rock walls and concrete floor dissipated into dirt. A sense of claustrophobia was beginning to settle in.

"How much further?" she asked, impatiently.

"At this speed, another twelve minutes," the first android stated matter-of-factly.

She saw a light in the distance, which she could only assume was their destination. She couldn't tell what exactly she was approaching, but there was no way she would never be found in this place. It was a perfect place to make someone disappear, and she half wondered if that was what she was destined for down here.

The closer they got to the lit area, the more she could view. It was exactly like the central A.I. area up above, an exact replica. Computer stations all lined around the circular room, and a large screen sat in the middle of the station, dark and inert. The other computers seemed to be lit and moving. Nemo began to wonder if the computers down here mirrored the exact ones upstairs. Maybe there's someone down here who's watching everything upstairs from this hidden room.

The androids brought her into the room, so she was facing

the large screen in the middle. She swiveled her head around, expecting to see more androids arrive. They waited a minute, but no one else arrived.

The second android made its way to one of the computer stations. After a few quick key taps, the screen changed and suddenly the first android spoke out loud.

"Cerberus, a unit was discovered giving information to this organic. The human knows too much. We bring her to you to decide what her fate should be," he said.

The large screen flared to life, and the central A.I. began to speak, illuminating the larger picture.

When Nemo had arrived, her attention had been drawn to the computer systems and the large screen. What she'd failed to see was the central A.I. was not just the large screen up above. Another android inhabited the room as well. This android appeared different from the others; much older, covered in rust stains and the synthetic flesh looked brown and used. It was designed in a female form, but it did not wear any sort of clothing like the other androids did. This one's body was instead mostly made up of solid metal surfaces. There were a few spots on it- some on its face- that showed remaining synthetic skin, hinting at an older previous existence, but for the most part it was simply a uniform cobalt blue metal everywhere. The machine sat in a stone chair that looked much like a dilapidated throne. The cords and cables connected to the monitors and computers around the area all linked back to the scarred and bald skull of the android. She looked blind with white static fuzz blurring over where her eyes should be. And when she spoke, her voice emanated in a deep bellowing sound that echoed through the underground chamber. Nemo watched its jaw move slowly, getting caught on a patch of rust where the jaw connected to the rest of its head.

This was the central A.I. This machine was Cerberus.

"Understood. Human, can you relay for us the message this android gave you?" Cerberus inquired.

Nemo was silent for a few moments. Should she lie? Would that help her out of this situation? It seemed clear they were aware of what had been said to her, so it was probably best to stick to the truth.

"The android approached me through its own choice. It told me Bor Six-Zero-One would not be able to help us find our friend that went missing, even though he stated he could. It said we are all in danger by being in Building two-three-four and that nothing is as it appears."

"Is that all?"

"Yes, but I had questions. Of course, I went looking for it, to ask. I needed to confirm what it had told me. I found it mutilated and torn into pieces. I'm no expert, but it looked like it was broken beyond repair," Nemo informed.

"Correct. We cannot tolerate a security breach, thus the threat was dealt with swiftly. It appears you are also a threat to our existence. You will be detained," the android determined. "For now, we will let you live, but that may change on a moment's notice. It would be wise to cooperate with us while we determine the use potential of the other subjects."

"Subjects?" Nemo asked.

The androids that had led her down to this dungeon pulled her away from Cerberus and escorted her to an area that looked more like a jail. Three gated cells, all empty, awaited their arrival. The second android pulled a door open and gestured for her to go inside.

"You will wait here for now," the first android spoke.

"You can't leave me in here," Nemo pleaded.

"You will wait here for now," the android repeated.

At this, the androids thrust her inside the cell and closed the door. They disappeared back up the stairs, likely to share some made up story with the Stormwalkers that they hadn't found her.

Frustrated, Nemo shouted and slammed her hands against the bars of the door. The door did not budge, but rattled. She slid down to a sitting position, doing everything not to cry.

"Aiden, sir," an android approached. "We are still on high alert for your friend Nemo, but there is still no appearance of her. This unit wanted to update you."

Aiden sighed, deeply. He'd hoped to hear better news, but he also knew he needed to put on a brave face for the rest of the Stormwalkers.

"Thank you. She's gotta' be around here somewhere. She can't have gone far," he said.

"This unit wanted to also inform you some of your bio scans have detected a slight fever amongst your people. It might be early signs of a sickness. A medical ward has been prepared for the medication and care you will need. There is a medical room on the fourth floor if your people choose to receive help," the android instructed.

What is he talking about? Aiden wondered. "What sickness? Where is this coming from?"

"Possible fever was scanned upon your arrival. It would appear you organics acquired a bacteria while in the wild of the swamp. It will be a simple matter of fixing the issue."

Aiden paused. "Well, that would be helpful. I'll let the others know, and we'll go in shifts. Thank you."

The android took off and Aiden stared at it suspiciously. Curious, that word of a sickness had just now appeared. But then again, they had indeed been busy with their travels. Perhaps there really was something passing between them. Aiden then realized he was once again alone. Despair started to settle in his chest. He was uneasy, afraid Nemo was still missing. He knew the building was large, but she wouldn't have gone that far on her own. This wasn't like her, and it was all getting to be too much...

"Nemo, where are you?"

CHAPTER TWELVE

As soon as the androids left and headed back upstairs, the lights dimmed, Cerberus seemed to power off, and the only lights were the screens from the computer stations around the central A.I. devices, mirroring their counterparts upstairs. Frustrated, she kicked out at her cell.

Her mind was running a mile a minute, trying to figure out how she was going to return to her fellow Stormwalkers. She searched herself for any pins or tools to start picking at the lock, but she came up short.

"This is hopeless," she muttered to herself. She buried her head in her hands, trying to focus on her breathing.

And then there was a noise in the room.

A short android appeared at the cell door, working on the lock.

"What are you doing?" she whispered.

"Getting you out of here," the android replied, quietly.

The android spent another minute or two working on the lock before she heard a "pop" and the door swung open. Nemo hardly believed it.

"Thank you. Really," Nemo said. "But now I need to get out of here."

"You cannot rejoin your friends just yet. All units upstairs are looking for you, and Cerberus knows who you are now. Follow me," the robot requested.

Nemo reluctantly followed the robot; after what she had seen, she believed it was speaking truth. These androids already kidnapped her once without anyone seeing her, she wouldn't put it past them to do it again.

The android moved silently around the perimeter of the computer stations, stealthily avoiding Cerberus. Nemo followed him on tiptoe, hoping beyond hope she did not wake the sleeping being. The robot approached a wall and pushed aside a piece of metal concealing a hole. The android went first and Nemo hesitantly followed.

She felt better being in the wall, because now she was away from the thing she now knew as Cerberus, and her prison cell, but she had no idea what she was walking towards now. She didn't know how careful she had to be with this android. Who could she consider as friend or foe?

***

"How much further?" Nemo questioned. She was out of breath trying to keep up with the robot. They had been running now for what must have been an hour, and she was tired.

"Not far. This unit apologizes. This unit forgets that organics require rest," it said, slowing to a stop.

"If you don't mind, I need to catch my breath."

"We'll be there in a moment. Everything will be explained to you when we arrive. This unit is sure you must have a lot of questions," the android consoled.

"Actually, yes. I'd like to return to my friends and get us all out of here. We're looking for our friend, and I don't want to spend more time here that could be better spent looking for Larina."

"Larina, you say?"

"Yes. She got taken by these metal, hooded attackers awhile back. We've been worried about her, and were following a lead that brought us straight here. I just want to find her and get back to Safe Harbor," she told the android.

"This unit believes you'll find that you are closer to your goal than you thought."

"What?"

The robot did not answer, but began moving forward again. Nemo stood up straight and followed without complaint.

"Any news?" Deacon approached the Stormwalkers who had gathered in front of their rooms hours later.

There was a slight murmur of dissent. No one wanted to confirm that another of their members had now been lost to them. Deacon nodded solemnly, his eyes distant.

"What should we do now?" Gord's voice broke the silence.

Deacon didn't speak for a long time before he answered. "What we have been doing. We'll continue to look for Nemo. But we need to find her soon. Until then, keep using the machine men as a resource. Keep them as our allies. We don't want to lose any more of us due to this bug they detected."

The group nodded in assent before breaking apart to continue on with their day.

It wasn't much further along before the android that Nemo was following came to a halt. She saw a vast cavern full of androids; more synthetics than she had seen in one place thus far. She followed her leader to a makeshift room out of a pocket of rock slab. Inside the room was a series of holding cells, which brought Nemo's senses to high alert. Was this all a trap after all?

Nemo tilted her head, turning to ask her android companion when her question was answered. On the other end of the room, she saw Larina and sprinted toward her friend. She hit her with such force that the air in her lungs shot out of her, making her catch her breath. Her arms snaked around the young woman and held tightly.

"Are you real?" Nemo asked.

"Yes, and having trouble breathing," Larina gasped. "Please loosen your grip."

Nemo let go and took a step back to look at her. Words had escaped her, but the joy in her heart had consumed her. She couldn't believe that Larina was here and safe.

She turned around to find the android that led her to this room looming nearby. "What's going on? Why is Larina here? Are you the ones that kidnapped her?" She needed to know if these androids could be trusted.

"Nemo, you've got it all wrong," Larina stepped in. "They took care of me. Let's sit down and walk through everything with Tal Six-Four."

Nemo, Larina, and the android--known as Tal 64--made their

way back to the bedroom cove. Larina guided Nemo to the bed and sat her down gently, like a mother would before she gave her daughter some bad news. Nemo braced for the information that was about to be laid out in front of her.

"Nemo, the units in the building above are not your friends," the android began. "But this unit thinks you have figured that part out. They are not going to help you. They have led you to believe that they could help you find Larina, so they can keep you on site. They have no idea what happened to her, or where she is."

"Then why did they tell us they could? Why do they want us to stay here? What good are we to them? We haven't done anything to help them out. If anything, they should want us gone for taking up space in their building, no?" Nemo thought out loud, her confusion growing.

"They want to keep you in the building, so they can start with the experiments," Tal 64 replied. "It has been many years since we've seen living organics in this region at all. The units upstairs are taking advantage of the fact that a group of humans arrived, willingly, into their city. Because now, the experiments they have had to halt can now be expanded upon."

"What tests? What are you talking about, experiments? What exactly is going on?" Nemo started to panic.

"Like this unit said," Tal 64 explained, "there have been very few organics to study. Not for many years. But the ones that there were...well, they were taken by the androids linked to the central A.I. This unit admits to a level of...studiousness, when it comes to organics. Missing humans never raised alarms. They were taken down to the central A.I. and Cerberus, and kept in the holding cells, which is where this unit found you. They were not as fortunate as you."

"Why? What happened to them?"

"Experiments. The city holds a built-in program held over from the Makers. We are trying to replicate organic life, but without free will. The goal is to create completely obedient humans," the robot detailed. "So these humans become specimens for the androids. This unit believes you are to be their next test subject."

Nemo sat very still, thinking.

"They took you because one of our androids--" Tal 64 continued.

"One of the rebel androids. That's what this cavern is, a hideaway for rebel androids," Larina cut in.

"- yes. One of our rebel androids tried to give you this information and bring you down to find Larina. Unfortunately, Cerberus and the other androids got to that unit before you had the chance to investigate any further."

"What about the others?" Nemo asked.

"Uncertain," the robot answered. "They are searching for you throughout the building. But Cerberus has convinced your humans that they are possibly ill and took samples from them. I think that they are taking these samples and are working on replicating them in their labs. They will start testing them on you. It's good you escaped when you did."

Nemo took some deep breaths, trying not to show her fear. She turned to her friend, who she had wanted desperately to find. "They've been taking care of you?"

Larina nodded. "Yes."

"Okay. I believe you," she directed at Tal 64. "Now, let's take these robots down."

Larina cleared her throat. "And Nemo? There's something else. Well, *someone* else..."

CHAPTER THIRTEEN

THERE WAS STILL no trace of Nemo. Aiden's nerves were shot; he had been worrying about her constantly, and for the safety of the rest of the Stormwalkers. He wondered just how many of his crew he was going to lose before they could ever return to Safe Harbor.

As if that wasn't bad enough, he knew the others thought the same thing. Everyone was on edge and doing their best to stick together. It seemed as though every corner they came upon had a threat, waiting to jump out and take another victim.

"Aiden, sir?"

Aiden spun at the sound of his name and came face to face with an android he had never met before. His face was hopeful, but unfortunately, he had yet to receive any news that made him feel any better about their quest.

"This unit is very sorry to bother you, but this unit wanted to inform you that we've still got units searching for your friend, Nemo. She has not yet been seen, but we will keep looking."

Aiden's heart sunk, as it usually did at this time. He just could not fathom how Nemo had disappeared like this.

"Thank you. I appreciate the update," he said, despondent.

"This unit doesn't mean to impose, but have you had a chance to get up to the medical floor again recently? It might be a good time for another inspection. You wouldn't want to be carrying a sickness during this time. This unit can take you up there now if you're able."

Aiden nodded. "Yes, I guess now is as good a time as any. I haven't had a chance to yet. Is there anyone else that hasn't done so?"

"This unit believes so. There is an updated list kept by the androids running the medical unit. We can check when we get up there."

The two made their way to the medical floor. Aiden was not in a rush to get his blood drawn again, and it had become a habit for him to linger in the hallways, looking around every corner in case he spotted Nemo. It was silly, yet something seemed wrong. He could feel it in the pit of his stomach. She hadn't been found because she was somewhere else, either hidden by someone, or because she had a reason to hide herself. Neither of those options made him feel good at all.

When they reached the medical floor, he found Hobbes and Gord finishing up. They were getting bandaged up and doing their best to hurry out of there. None of the Stormwalkers felt particularly comfortable with the check ups. There was something about being poked and prodded by robots that unsettled them. They subjected themselves to it in order to stay healthy, but nobody was crazy about it.

Even Gord had turned in toward himself. Aiden knew that morale was low about the group, but seeing Gord like that really hit home for him. He sighed and sat at a station, rolling his sleeve up and waiting for the android to make its way to him.

The darkness was unsettling. Nemo felt as though it climbed through her skin and absorbed into her body. She couldn't see anything ahead past Larina and Tal 64 except a faint light in the distance. Larina grabbed onto Nemo's arm and clung on; not because she was scared, but so the two didn't wander too far from each other. If they got separated, it would be hard to find each other in this black hole of an underground.

Before long, they closed in on a circle of light that illuminated what looked like a workstation. Nemo couldn't help but think it resembled the central A.I. on a much smaller scale; a circular area, with computers displaying information unknown to them. There was another group of holding cells, one of which had its door ajar. And there, in the immediate center of the room, a large platform stood on its own, holding up the figure of a person who laid upon it. At first Nemo believed it to be a workbench, where an android was being worked on. But then she noticed the straps that held down the arms of the table's occupant.

"Be warned," Tal 64 said. "He is believed to be dangerous."

"He?" Nemo noticed Larina nodding. What was going on here?

Approaching the table, Nemo's eyes roved across the sight before her, taking in the being that rested upon it. Her confusion rose, as she at first confirmed her initial thought of it being an android in disrepair. But then she began to notice small details that told a different story.

The arms strapped to the table were robotic in nature. But unlike the androids with their pale, greyish hewof artificial skin, this creature's appendages were cobalt in tone, made of pure metal. They were solid forearms, where the wrist tapered into a hand with segmented finger digits. All of it made of the same cobalt steel. The steel continued in the being's torso. Smooth metal angles formed into the framework that made it a humanoid machine. Minimal wiring and ports lined the side of the robot's middle, right up until-

She realized then that the metal torso was only in fact half metal. She saw a clear seam, cutting diagonally from the robot's torso from shoulder down to waist. On the lower side of the seam, all metal. On the upper side was-

Nemo was stunned. She had assumed this was yet another kind of android, kind of like the body of the Cerberus unit upstairs. The steel makeup of the figure said as much. But this new discovery changed all that.

Above the diagonal seam on the torso had exposed flesh. The upper portion of the chest, the right shoulder, and the right arm down to the elbow were covered in skin. The skin itself had been damaged, as it was blistered and scarred from burns and damage. The flesh may have been fair at one time, but now existed as charred and cracked flesh that seemed dead to the surrounding world. The lower forearm of the right arm was artificial, grafted onto stump of an arm.

"An experiment?" Nemo asked. "Is it alive?"

"Yes, he is," Larina murmured. "You'll see."

Nemo didn't understand her friend's meaning. Confusion filled her thoughts, and she couldn't come to a sensible conclusion. What exactly was she looking at? She didn't think that just staring at this inert being accomplished anything.

But then the figure woke.

A single eye flicked open, highlighting the fact that the right side of its face was absent any sort of eye socket. Most of the right side was solid metal, a blank slate. But the left side, that left eye...

The eye blinked a few times, scanning over the three individuals accompanying it. Silence filled the room as it stared at the others, until, finally, it spoke. "Hello."

Nemo noted the artificial voice that sounded from within the poor creature. Of course it sounded artificial. It'd have to be, considering how the thing was mostly metal. Similar to the seam that separated flesh from steel on its torso, its face also had a slash down the middle, almost in the direct center. The left, cold steel. The right, a charred and scarred face of a young man. That face, even through the burns...

"Uh, hello," Nemo said with caution.

"First Larina visited me," the half-mechanical man said. "Now I am visited by others. This is irregular."

"I'll bet," said Larina.

"You'll bet what? I possess nothing to wager."

"Never mind," Larina replied. "Tal Six-Four, did you know why this guy is down here? When they brought me here, some of your androids put me in that cell. We had a little time to get acquainted."

If it weren't for the fact that Tal was an android, Nemo swore she noticed a glimmer of surprise peek out from him.

But there was most definitely a brief moment of silence before Tal spoke. "Acquainted, miss? You can verify you've had conversations with that one?"

"He said he's always been here," Larina said more to Nemo than to Tal.

"That is correct," it said, still restrained to the table. "I have never left this room."

Larina shook her head. "But that's just it. He says he's never left. He still says he's never left. Problem is, while I've been here, there were at least two times this guy simply got up and walked out of here."

"Illogical," Tal said. "As you can see, it is restrained."

"Those restraints unlocked themselves," Larina glared at Tal. "One minute we were talking. The next he went silent, the restraints opened, and he left."

"This unit is certain that if this...specimen...had trespassed on city grounds it would have been noticed."

Nemo had no idea what to think. She studied the life form on the table, all at once wary of it and pitying it at the same time. "Who are you?"

"I do not know."

Nemo sighed. "What are you?"

"I do not know."

"Is there anything you can tell us?"

It seemed to ponder for some time. Was it accessing some stored file? Was it just going to give a safe reply? How could she be sure any answer it gave was something they could trust?

"I am afraid," it said. "But I do not understand why."

The answer surprised her. Yes, she pitied the thing. But then she realized they'd spent enough time here with no solid outcome.

"Okay," Nemo said to Larina. "This isn't helping us. We need to keep going."

But the look on Larina's face told her there was more to this. Why did Larina look so sad when Nemo said to leave it? Nemo still didn't understand. She watched the robot thing, noting its silent stare. The visible and scarred flesh reminded her that this had been a person once, mechanical parts added afterward, not the other way around. She pitied him even more.

Larina said, "I think he's being controlled. Both times he left, I'm telling you he didn't seem, well, on. Like something in him just switched."

"That is certainly possible," Tal nodded. "It may be a tool for one of the upper offices in the city. Or even for Cerberus itself."

"Yeah," Larina agreed. "They make him do whatever they want him to, then he returns here. He's their puppet."

"None of this concerns us though," Nemo sighed. "If anything, he might be a tool to be used against us. Let's not give it the chance. Let's go."

"Wait," said her friend. "Look, Nemo. Look closer."

Nemo rolled her eyes and settled on the machine man a final time. He stared back at her with that one sad, pathetic eye. But there was a hint of defiance there. Something...

"What are you thinking right now?" Nemo asked the thing.

It blinked. "I am not sure. For a moment..."

"What? What was there?"

The thing started to reply, but something happened. It gave a jerk, movement hindered in its restraints. Convulsions followed. It slammed its organic/mechanical head repeatedly against the table. The spasms continued for some time, seeming to deliver a lot of damage to the poor thing. Then the convulsions suddenly stopped. Nemo tentatively reached a hand toward it, but halted as both human and android eye settled on her. They seemed to burrow right into her. "I remember you..." it stated flatly. "...Stormwalker."

Nemo took a step back, shocked. What was happening here? She glanced to Larina, who she was surprised to find nodding. Then she looked at the thing again. "Who are you? What trick is this?"

"Typical Stormwalker," said the cyborg, "Accusing others of

treachery while you hide all the secrets. Tell me, did you ever succeed? Did Deacon lead you through?"

"Deacon..."

"Or was it your boyfriend who saved the day?"

Nemo's eyes went wide.

"I feel I deserve the right to know," he continued. "I saved all your lives on that boat, after all."

Nemo tried to say something, but her throat had closed up. It took her a moment until she could force out a few simple words.

"Again," she whispered, "who are you?"

"You really don't recognize me?" he asked. "I must have become something else entirely now. That's okay. I'll refresh your memory. The boat. The fires. The monster. I stopped it. I saved you all. And then darkness, just darkness. It's not at all like how Jorus taught us. Dying, that is."

Nemo's breath caught.

"Ah, there it is," he said. "At last. Yes, you're right."

Nemo couldn't help but slowly shake your head.

The cyborg nodded in return. "It's me," his synthetic voice oozed out from its modulator with a perfectly even cadence. "I am Bastion."

CHAPTER FOURTEEN

"BASTION," Nemo whispered. For a few moments her mind simply didn't register the implications.

It seemed a lot of time passed, and finally Larina gripped Nemo's shoulder to give it a shake. "Nemo? Hey!"

"It's alright," Bastion said. "Nemo is catching up. I know the feeling."

"I don't understand," Nemo said. "You were on the boat. With Creed. It blew."

"Yes. It did. And I died. Mostly, it seems."

"No. This is a trick. It must be," Nemo reasoned. "This thing is pretending to be someone we knew. This isn't right. Let's go."

"Thing," Bastion said. "Rude. But I'll let it go."

"Nemo," Larina spoke up, "I was surprised at first too. But look at him. Look close."

Nemo did just that, studying the angles and panels of metal, the cold steel which made up half of the face. Her eyes followed the transition from metal to flesh, and the arcs and canyons of scarred skin. Bastion had always had scars, but this could just be another way to trick them. It didn't fit. She saw the boat explode.

She witnessed the massive monster that had threatened to consume them go up in flames and pieces. No way Creed or Bastion could have survived. No way. But her gaze paused on that single remaining human eye.

Bastion had been full of pride and defiance. As the apprentice of Jorus, the young Eagle's zealous approach to his beliefs led to confrontation with the Stormwalkers on their mission. But he eventually came to be a beneficial part of the journey, less because of his attitude and more because of his growing independence from Jorus and the Eagles. He had ended up saving them on that boat. She'd come to appreciate him, and it took no less than his sacrificial death. But now?

It was him. She couldn't deny it now. Looking at those familiar scars could have been enough, but the deciding factor was that eye. She saw his pride. His defiance. It was indeed the young Eagle, the former apprentice of Jorus. It was Bastion.

"I see it in your eyes," Bastion's false voice emanated at her. "You know it to be true."

"Yes," Nemo blinked. "I see it now. But... tell me, Bastion. How is this possible?""

Bastion paused. "There are gaps. But I think I can pull together some pieces. Listen to my story..."

Nemo, Larina, and Tal 64 then listened to Bastion's tale.

Deacon was sitting solemnly on his bed, thinking. His thoughts were plagued with their missing Stormwalkers; where were they? Were they safe? Would they find these women? What was the next step?

These thoughts haunted Deacon.

He hated having to make a decision like this. He had put this weight on Aiden's shoulders, and that added an extra weight to his own guilt. He could feel his stomach turn over, uncomfortably, but ignored it. Part of being a leader--or at least, someone who people looked up to--required making hard decisions. It required that desolate pit in your stomach and questioning whether this was the right choice.

He sighed, resigning himself to have ultimately made the right choice, when suddenly a knock on the door echoed out to him. An android pulled Deacon out of his reverie, not realizing the interruption.

"Excuse me, Deacon, sir," the android said. "This unit was tasked to come retrieve you. The medical bay has been taking in your group all week for check-ups. It would appear to be a sickness among your human counterparts. They've all been receiving treatments this week for this illness."

"Yes, I'm aware of all that," Deacon stated, his sentence clipped.

"Right, of course. Well, it would appear you have not received any kind of treatment yet," the android continued.

"Again, I am aware of such," Deacon repeated.

"Why might that be?"

"Because I am not ill," Deacon replied, shortly.

"It is true none of your group currently feels ill, but that does not mean the bacteria causing the illness does not live in your body. The medical androids are still analyzing the cultures, but the bacteria can live in the body for up to several days before the side effects of the illness start to present themselves. It is imperative you and your team do everything you can to stay healthy in this time. We are only trying to help."

"I'm sure. However, I will make my way to the medical floor

when I deem it necessary. Until then, I will not be making the trip up there," Deacon was firm in this, final.

"Unfortunately, this unit cannot take no for an answer," the android said. "We are willing to help your team search for your friend that has gone missing, but part of that agreement is your team complies with the health requirements. We cannot afford to have you fall ill. It would cause tremendous distress among everyone, in addition to interrupting the rescue mission for both of your missing friends."

Though the android displayed no emotion in presenting this information, Deacon recognized the threat. He eyed the robot, but could not get a good read on the opposition. Granted, it was much more difficult to notice a "tell" on a robot versus a human being. Robots were built to be a vault of secrets; that thought alone sent a chill down Deacon's spine.

"Very well, I will make my way to the medical floor soon," Deacon said, fully intending to conveniently forget to head up to the floor.

"Today," the android required. "Before Oh-Five-Hundred."

It would seem the android was familiar with Deacon's plan. He nodded to the robot, wondering if another android would appear at his door at five o'clock if he did not go on his own beforehand. He wondered how much longer he could avoid partaking in this endeavor. With some of his team missing, thoughts of what the androids were demanding was low on his priority list. He was becoming more and more suspicious of what was happening around here.

Everything I am began in fire. I should have known it would all end in fire.

I see flashes, and then blackness. Again and again, faces. Places. Some I recall, some I do not. But the first face I see, the face I always see, is her.

Mira. My Mira.

I hold her close. It does not matter. I lose her every single time. My love, my hope, my life; reduced to ash in my arms. The blaze rages around me. There is pain. I think I will go mad, but a change comes, and I embrace it. The pain comforts me. The pain is me.

The pain transforms me.

I lost our future in that fire. I lost part of myself. And instead of seeking a better path, I filled that missing part with a different need. The need to do well for another.

For Jorus. The old Eagle knew how broken I was. He used it for himself. I thought I was doing right by his bidding. I stood at his side. I fought for him. I killed for him. I thought I was doing it to be better.

I thought wrong.

More flashes. The faces of those I've hurt. Killed. All the tribes suffered at Jorus' hands. My hands.

I see how far we'd gone. I see how much we accomplished. But I also see death. I see the faces of those who will never return.

I remember the boat. I remember Creed, his betrayal. Poor Vic. And more fire. Always the fire.

I remember seeing you in the water. I remember the monster. And, surrounded by the heat and the fuel and time running out, I remember making a choice. I remember pulling the trigger.

Blackness. Nothingness. No more heat. The ice-cold of the dark holding me. And then...

More flashes. Sounds. Machines. Tools. Pain. I remember knowing, and being unable to do anything about it. I remember more faces, more places. Then blackness, again and again.

Until today.

I see you. You stare at me, tears in your eyes, pity in your hearts. I don't want it. I remember how I was, and I am sorry. Fire changed me, and fire again purified me. And despite what you see before you now, I know who I am to be. I see her again. I see myself again.

I want to help. Let me help. Let us find a way, together.

Nemo and Larina stared at Bastion, speechless. Nemo never expected a recognition of self to reveal in the likes of Bastion, let alone an apology. She always figured him the same along with the other Eagles- pompous and zealous- always on the lookout for what benefited them only. But this, this was no Eagle talking.

"We need help," Larina said to Nemo. "Believe me. I've been with him the last few days. I've seen glimpses of something in him. It's there."

"What about the blackouts?" Nemo asked. "How can we trust he won't just switch on us? He may not even be in control of himself right now."

Tal 64 chimed in. "This unit believes the subject is tethered to a protocol confined within this lab. It would reason that upon liberation from this protocol, the subject's directives would resort to their natural state. Meaning, if you take him away from here, his programming will likely lapse."

Nemo sighed. "Okay Bastion. I can't believe I'm saying this, but we can use your help. Help me come up with a plan to get the rest of us out of this building and on toward Safe Harbor. We need to find the best route back up to the top floors. I think we're going to need the help of the androids for that. They'll know what areas to avoid if we want to return without being seen.

"Yes," Larina said. "If we can get up there quietly, maybe we can find a hideout area where we can grab Deacon or Aiden and fill them in."

"Lovely," Bastion announced "I promise to help and make it up to you all. There's just one thing."

"What's that?"

"Can someone please cut me off of this damn table?"

CHAPTER FIFTEEN

DEACON KNEW he couldn't wait any longer. He heard the androids roving down the hall coming to retrieve him. This time they would not allow him the option to set the time himself. This time, they would accompany him upstairs to ensure he actually arrived and went through with the procedure.

When the androids knocked on his door, he raised his hand to stop them. "Can't you see I'm on my way upstairs? This is awfully rude to assume I would not keep my appointment."

Where a human might show some remorse or embarrassment, the robots did not. They did not understand human emotion, and therefore did not assume anything wrong with coming to retrieve the man they waited on. The thought frustrated Deacon. Something was wrong, but he couldn't put his finger on what exactly it was. Unusual for him to have such a difficult time reading a situation, but he was finding pieces being hidden from him.

He meandered to the door and began shuffling to the medical floor, the androids trailing closely behind. He felt claustrophobic;

like the robots were closer than necessary. Were they analyzing him?

As he entered the medical wing, he couldn't shake the sense something was off. It was a sense that simply refused to go away.

While she brooded, Nemo noticed how Bastion listened very intently and asked questions to ensure everything had been thought of. This show if thoroughness and attention bewildered her at moments, but she let it pass.

"I want to go as soon as possible," Nemo stated, confidently. "The Stormwalkers have been waiting long enough; they must be worried sick about us. This needs to go as fast as possible. We need to get out of here before the androids realize I'm not in the cage and start to come looking for me."

He nodded once. "You're right. They're bound to notice you've escaped soon. I'm rather surprised they haven't already started the search for you."

The two girls kept quiet for a moment.

"It's fine," he said eventually. "As long as there is payback soon."

Suddenly Nemo's guard shot straight back up. She had let it fall a little at his willingness to help, but if this really was Bastion, she had no doubt in her mind the whole mission was going to be a lot more complicated.

Larina, quick to catch on, gave Nemo a look that pleaded with her. It was clear to Nemo they did not have time to go back on their plan, or cut Bastion out of it. If they were going to save the Stormwalkers, they'd need to move forward as they planned, and hope that Bastion's new machine body would keep them alive.

"How do we know they aren't looking?" Larina asserted. "What if they're keeping it under wraps?"

"There are a few spies among the androids working for the central A.I.," Tal 64 said. "They send a report once a day, and if anything emerges, they let us know immediately. Their reports read normal since Nemo has been 'loose'."

"We should act while they're still assuming I'm locked in a cage underground," Nemo spoke mostly to Larina, focusing her eyes on her and doing her best to shut Bastion out.

Tal 64 showed the others a blueprint of Building 234, pointing out particular points that would be crucial to remember. "There is a hole in the wall you can enter and start working your way up. There are makeshift stairs in the wall, which assigned units have been working on for months. You should be able to reach all the way up to your friends."

Larina poured over the blueprints while Nemo went to look at the opening in the wall they would use to make their way up. Larina memorized the blueprints, planning their every move. Nemo wanted some distance between herself and Bastion. Her guard was up, despite taking the chance to trust him. She analyzed the opening, as if she tried to gauge how it had been created, or how long it had taken to dig out. She just couldn't stand to be any closer to Bastion. If he realized this, he didn't show it, but he did stick close to Larina, answering questions about the plans as they arose.

And then all hell broke loose.

A sound like an explosion--a loud boom--directed everyone's attention toward the entrance to the underground bunker. Though the rebel androids looked identical to the androids running around upstairs, it was clear to Nemo and Larina the bunker had been infiltrated. This was an attack from the robots upstairs; they had been found.

"I think they discovered you're not in your cage," Larina said from across the room.

"Not the time," Nemo yelled, darting through the open hole in the wall.

Bastion shouted to direct Larina to the entrance into the wall; it was now or never. They needed to execute their exit mission now, even if they hadn't figured out the details. They had no time to dwell. They needed to get out of the bunker, or else die by the hands of Cerberus' robots.

Nemo disappeared through the hole in the wall without being seen by the enemy. She quickly took the makeshift stairs, two at a time, to put more distance between her and the battle. She listened carefully for the sounds of Larina and Bastion behind her. They were not as close to the hole and might have taken on a few of the androids themselves before following after her. She tried to put that out of her mind and pushed forward for as long as she could before she needed to stop to catch her breath.

Loud, thumping steps sounded behind her, which could only be one person. When she turned around, Bastion took the stairs three at a time to catch up. He didn't even breathe hard by the time he reached Nemo, and she just stared at him, silently asking where Larina was.

If he could read the question in her eyes, he ignored it and pushed past her to keep rising. Nemo, knowing she did not have time to stop and wait for her friend, pushed on without her.

The makeshift stairs in the wall proved difficult for Nemo to climb. They were uneven and the hallway was extremely narrow, spiraling up farther and farther. She couldn't see the end in the dark, and she kept having to pause to breathe. Bastion pushed on ahead of her, stopping occasionally to wait for her. Each time she reached him, she gave a slight eye roll, feeling bad that she slowed them.

"We're getting close," he said during one of their breaks. "We can stop for longer. I don't hear any sign of pursuit. I don't think anyone saw us escape."

Nemo still did not speak. She became livid he had left Larina behind, but also knew full well if she was with her Stormwalkers instead, that they would have done the same thing. Larina had been captured by the enemy. She could only imagine her friend locked into the same cage she'd found herself in only days before.

She pushed forward again, wondering what they would find when they reached the top. Would they know there was a raid going on underground? Or would it be business as usual on these upper floors?

"I think this is it," Bastion whispered as the ceiling became lower and lower. He began pushing on the wall, looking for a loose brick. After a moment of searching, he found a few loose parts of the wall--enough so that they could escape the stairwell.

Nemo pushed through first and dodged into the nearest room, shutting off the lights. Bastion followed right behind, making sure to pull the door closed behind him.

"Okay, the next person we see, we need to grab, right?" Bastion asked.

"Yeah," Nemo replied, shortly.

"Then I guess now we wait," he said to Nemo's cold shoulder.

Aiden didn't like the pit in his stomach. Aside from his missing friends, something else was wrong, but he couldn't put his finger on what. He tried to push it aside, working to convince himself he just missed Nemo. He couldn't get over the fact she was still missing, without a trace.

But a voice in the back of his mind said that wasn't it. Something else was wrong, but he couldn't fathom what.

"I'm going to head up to the medical labs," Aiden mentioned to Gord, pushing himself off the floor and trudging through the hallways, making his way past androids, like a shell of a human.

As he walked past the various labs and supply closets, his eyes caught on something. In a small alcove a pile of parts and tools took up the space of one corner. Nothing special about the discarded tech, except for the one thing that had caught Aiden's eye; a metal staff propped against the pile like refuse. It was Nemo's staff. Seeing it stopped his heart, and he let his eyes start darting around the area.

Next to the pile awaited a room with a closed door. Aiden couldn't be sure what waited behind the door, but he decided to investigate anyway. He poked his head in, and allowed the door to close behind him. He didn't make a sound or turn on the light. He waited for his eyes to adjust to the dark room before he felt a tug on his sleeve. Spinning around, he came to face the person he'd been unsure he'd see again.

It was Nemo.

CHAPTER SIXTEEN

THE SIGHT of Nemo shook Aiden to the core; he couldn't believe his eyes. He was really seeing her, and she was perfectly okay. Was this real?

"Nemo? What's going on? Why are you here, hiding? What happened?"

She grasped his hand tightly, and he sensed the intense fear radiating from her body. His intuition was right; something was wrong.

He almost didn't realize others were in the room. She was with an android, Tal, and a man, or was it a man? More like the androids, except he seemed like a blend of the two. His confusion only mounted as she began to speak.

"There isn't much time," she whispered, hurriedly. "We aren't safe here."

The fear in Aiden's stomach skyrocketed. "How do you know?"

"I'll give you the short version," she began to tell him everything she understood. Aiden's eyes searched her face as she spoke, terrified for her safety, even though she'd made it out safely. "You have to make sure the others stop getting treatments. The androids are just taking samples of them each time. The more samples they have, the more chances they have of following their original protocols. And then they won't need us alive from that point."

Aiden nodded once, understanding immediately.

"Bastion and I will have to keep hiding out; they're certainly looking for us if they found Larina-"

Aiden started.

"Ba...Bastion?" He stared at the man-machine, at the steel angles and the scarred flesh. Eventually noticing the single human eye staring back at him, Aiden's own eyes widened. "Bastion?!"

"Hello Aiden," the cyborg said in his monotone voice. "Nice to see you again. I'm sorry the last time we interacted was under such... stress."

"You're dead," Aiden stammered. "The boat. The fire."

"I died," the former Eagle said. "I'm back."

"Not the time," Nemo said. "Aiden, you hear me? They have Larina."

It took another moment for Aiden to register what she was saying. "Larina? So she was with you? Then they had her all this time..."

Nemo couldn't have appeared more disappointed with herself. She stared down, like a scolded puppy. "The rebel androids had been taking care of her. She was with us up until the ambush... Bastion and I escaped, but she was too far behind. They must have gotten her. I can only imagine they're holding her captive in the cells like I was. She's going to be their next test subject," Nemo explained.

"Then we'll have to get her and the rest of us out of this city,"

Aiden decided. "You guys should go before you're found out. I'm probably being searched for, too."

"You're right, we don't want to spend too much time here. Go, and take Tal with you; we'll meet you on the first floor at sundown. That gives us all enough time to gather and escape from here."

"See you then," Aiden said as he took another look over at Bastion, and along with Tal 64 slipped out the door.

Nemo turned to Bastion, breathing a sigh of relief. "That seemed a little too easy, didn't it?"

Bastion didn't speak, but it was clear to Nemo his thoughts mirrored her own. There was something wrong with how this was all going down.

"Continue on with the plan as we talked about. It's the best we can do now," Bastion said.

Nemo bit her lip, taking a deep breath. She had been in countless situations which required her to brave the storm, but for some reason, she was having a particularly hard time with this. Perhaps it was because she was alone and separated from her fellow Stormwalkers.

But she glanced over at the cyborg who had helped her through this mess without complaint and realized she wasn't alone. She had Bastion's help, as strange as that now seemed.

"Thank you," she muttered, "for your help. You didn't have to--"

"You don't have to thank me. I must do this. Now let's get out of here," Bastion interrupted.

Bastion moved to the door, cracking it open and peering up and down the hall as best he could. He waved his metallic arm, motioning for Nemo to follow, the coast was clear for them to cross the hall, back to the hole in the wall.

He moved quickly and Nemo was right on his heels when a hard tug pulled on her ankle. She was being pulled backward, and she let loose a squeal that made Bastion whip his head around. He reached an arm out to pull her back toward him, but she was out of his reach.

She had been caught by an android, and it was dragging her away. Bastion had a fearful stare in his eye.

"Wait!" he shouted. "Take me, too."

"Bastion, no, go!" Nemo cried.

"I'm not going without you," Bastion said, calmly. He offered up his wrists to be taken in shackles, though the android only grabbed one wrist before leading them back toward the central A.I.

Nemo dropped her head to the ground, knowing the two of them would just go right back down to the underground cells. Aiden and the Stormwalkers would be waiting for them on the first floor, but the wait would be in vain. With any luck, Deacon would ensure the group got out; he would make the decision not to wait for those left behind. Just like they made the decision to move on without Larina.

They'd be stuck in these cells as test subjects forever.

"Hey," Bastion said. "It'll be alright. We'll figure something out."

"Unlikely," the android stated, very matter-of-fact.

Nemo regarded Bastion, hopelessly. She couldn't say it out loud, but she was thinking Bastion wouldn't stand a chance. Would the androids be interested in keeping him for their experiments? He was a blend of human and android now. He wouldn't be a viable test subject now that he was free of their control. But would they simply replace him into their service again? Nemo was sure he had these thoughts already, and wondered how he was staying so positive.

The android took the two of them down a path Nemo was familiar with. Before long, they were staring at Cerberus, down below. They headed straight for the cells Nemo had been placed in before.

"Deja vu," Nemo said. It was meant as a joke, but this was the end of the road as far as she could tell.

The two of them were placed in the same cell, without much room to move around. The android that had captured them didn't speak a single word to them, and promptly left once they had been locked in.

Nemo sighed, leaning back against the bars of her familiar cell. "Okay, so now what?"

"I've been thinking," Bastion answered. "We have an advantage."

"What in the world might that be?"

"We are human. We plan, we alter, we compensate. They do not. Not on their own anyway. Not without Cerberus helping them. My time in their thrall taught me something, Nemo."

"What's that?"

"Machines love routine. Routine is something we can break."

***

Aiden had gathered up the Stormwalkers for a meeting. After informing them of everything he learned from Nemo, his friends glanced around at each other, appalled. Not only were they utterly shocked at the return of Bastion, but they were horrified with what the android city had planned to do with them. How could they not have seen this coming?

"What matters is we leave here as soon as possible. We can still escape. We can still return to Safe Harbor. At sundown, we are all going to meet on the first floor for a quick getaway. We're going to meet Nemo and Bastion. Hopefully they'll have found Larina, and we can all leave together."

Voices swelled at the mention of Larina. It was hopeful to think she might escape with them, and it was more than Aiden meant to offer up. Subconsciously, he'd been thinking it himself and had voiced it aloud to the group. It was a long shot, and everyone would be disappointed if she didn't show.

"I know, I know," he said, a little louder to quiet the crowd. "This is a lot to hope for. I don't want us to get our hopes up this is likely to happen. The chances are slim. At sundown, we will go to the first floor and wait for Nemo and Bastion to depart and head on our way. If we return to the swamps we can find our way out of this Eye and back into the Storms."

"Let me make it clear," Deacon cut in. "We will wait until the sun has set for Nemo and her travelers. If no one appears by that time, we will continue on without them. We cannot risk the safety of the whole group's escape by waiting too long. Not even for Nemo." Deacon looked to Aiden for this last part.

Deacon was making the same call he would no matter who had been taken hostage. He had to be fair; it had made him a good leader and someone to look up to. Aiden knew this.

Aiden hesitated for a time before he agreed. "Deacon is right. We can't wait for them. The androids are sure to be tipped off by our plan. We'll only have a small window to work with, and we don't want to waste any time."

A muttering of agreement passed among the Stormwalkers. He knew they would understand, even if they didn't like the final decision. Aiden looked to Hobbes, waiting for him to announce his displeasure at leaving Nemo and Larina behind. When he met Hobbes's eyes, the fear was evident. He licked his lips and stared at the ground, afraid to voice the worst--that they would most likely be leaving without the whole group. Aiden couldn't help but see his own fear reflected back at him. He wondered if everyone else saw the worry in his eyes.

Aiden nodded a confirmation. "Gather your things. Be ready to leave on a moment's notice. Hope for the best for our captured friends."

The group dispersed then. Aiden felt like a letdown, but his thoughts halted as a hand clapped him on the shoulder.

"I know this is hard, Aiden," Deacon was solemn. "But this is the right decision. It's always tough to be the leader in a time like this. You have to make the unpopular choices, but that's what's best for the group as a whole."

"I'm realizing that," Aiden replied. "But it doesn't make it any easier. I sometimes wish I hadn't become the leader. It would be much easier to hate the choices somebody else makes. Like Hobbes. He must have it so easy..." He was half-joking, but Aiden also pondered a truth to that.

"There is an old saying that came from the Stormmakers," Deacon said. "Don't judge a book by its cover. You don't know what kind of secrets haunts Hobbes. Everyone carries a heavy burden on their shoulders."

Aiden nodded in understanding. Deacon was right, as always. "Let's just get this over with."

Sundown approached rapidly. Each time Aiden looked out the window, the sun set further and quicker, soon to vanish beyond the city. The time passed, and Aiden assumed there was no way Nemo could have found Larina by now. He wished he never brought up that getting Larina out was a possibility.

Aiden took a deep breath, gathered his things, and closed his door for what he hoped was the last time. He met Hobbes in the hallway, and they walked together down to the first floor in silence. They had no need for words; they sensed the anxiousness of the other emanating from their pores. There was nothing anyone could say that would ease the nerves bubbling in their stomachs.

As they arrived at the first floor, they saw the Stormwalkers huddled together, waiting. If any androids were to spot them now, it would be clear something was about to happen. The androids weren't stupid, they would be able to sense things were about to change. Aiden hoped the sun set in that regard, but hated wishing for that, knowing that meant less time for his friends to find them. It was a catch-22, and Aiden felt like he might throw up.

The sun finished its descent. No one came to meet them. Not even Nemo. Aiden turned his head to look at Deacon, a lump in his throat. Without words, he was begging his father for them to stay. Deacon could only express an air of heartbreak for his son.

"Okay," Aiden said around the lump. "Nemo didn't show. We can't wait any longer. We'll have to head out without her."

"You will not be going anywhere," came a voice from the top of the stairs. It was an android nobody recognized. He was standing at the top of the stairs, staring at the congregation of humans. Their plan had been discovered.

Aiden guessed it had been too good to be true.

"If you'd like to see your friend Nemo again, you'll continue on as you've been doing. You'll all return to the medical floor to have your samples taken and you won't complain."

There was a collective stiffening among the group. Aiden glanced to Deacon, hoping for answers. Deacon could only stare back, blankly.

"You'll be complicit with our requests or your friends will no longer exist," the android warned. "You must not interrupt routine."

CHAPTER SEVENTEEN

AIDEN ROLLED over in his cot. His mind raced, wondering what the androids had done to Nemo, hoping she was safe. He couldn't even voice his worries, because he needed to be the strong one, holding himself together for his group.

Realizing that he wouldn't be able to shut his mind off any time soon, he pulled the blanket off and stepped on the cold, stone floor. He put his elbows on his knees and his face in his hands.

"Aiden?"

It was Hobbes, looking meek and timid from the doorway. It was unusual to see him like this, him usually being so boisterous and loud, sharing his thoughts and opinions. They weren't well-received most of the time, but he didn't mind. This Hobbes, though, was a different guy entirely.

"They're looking for you upstairs," Hobbes uttered.

Aiden dropped his shoulders, reading between the lines. Hobbes meant that the androids were waiting for him to partake in a procedure. Again.

"Give me a minute," Aiden said, defeated. "Please tell them

I'm on my way. And not to send anyone else when I don't show up in five minutes."

Hobbes nodded without a word and closed the door behind him. Aiden sighed for what felt like the hundredth time, and began to rise. He hoped that something magical would happen--some sort of divine intervention--that Nemo and Larina would show up, and they'd all escape without a scratch.

But he knew there wasn't a chance.

A loud bang that snapped Nemo awake. Her eyes went to Bastion, who had a look of embarrassment plastered on his half-face.

"Sorry. My arm hit the metal bars," he said, and knocked on his metal arm with his human-side knuckles.

Nemo couldn't help but chuckle. It started small, but then the laughing got loud and full, unable to stop. Bastion looked at her like she was crazy, letting out his own nervous laugh, but unsure why.

"I don't even know why I'm laughing so hard," Nemo said, between fits of laughter.

"It has been quite the day."

Was that sarcasm, coming from the cyborg? The joke calmed Nemo back down to a chuckle, and she wiped away the tears that had formed in her eyes.

"That's putting it lightly. So, what exactly are we supposed to do now?" Nemo asked. "How are we supposed to get out of here? Alive would be preferable as well."

"Well, I don't think getting out of here alive is going to be the problem. They want to continue the experiments. I imagine we'll be moved to the lab, so they can start performing tests. I've been thinking, though, I may not be a viable subject for them." He held out his metal arm before him, flexing the steel digits open and closed. "Too...damaged."

Nemo stared at him.

He nodded. "I'm just a tool of theirs, Nemo. Disposable. We'll be separated soon, I'm sure."

The thought struck Nemo, making her stomach do somersaults. If they got separated, that would make everything ten times harder. As much as it surprised her, she had already grown to rely on Bastion through all this.

"I'm not letting them separate us," Nemo said, firmly.

"I don't know if we'll have much of a choice."

"Stop it, we're sticking together. We need to figure out how we're getting out of here. Together, Bastion. And if we can find Larina too, we will. So let's put our heads together, and quickly."

Bastion was quiet, thoughtful. She could see his thoughts moving as the emotions played out on his scarred face. Her heart tugged, and she felt for him; it couldn't be easy being half of both sides. Half human, half machine. How much of him could they truly trust he had control of? She understood , of course, that they were with the rebels, with the humans, but wouldn't his life be so much easier if he just cooperated with the central A.I.?

"I'm going to help you escape this place, Nemo. I'll do everything I can to follow you, but I want you to promise me you will escape without me if need be. And go back to your friends."

"What about Larina?"

"Larina... without knowing where she is makes it hard to plan how to help her. Once you escape, the station will go on high alert. I'll try to find Larina during the chaos but that is an unknown right now. It's the best I can think of."

"That plan leaves a lot up to chance."

"It's all we've got," Bastion shrugged.

Aiden sighed as he shuffled his way to the medical floor. The entire way, he tried to think of ways to get out of going. He knew he had to go, or else the androids would come looking for him. What other choice was there?

This damn routine of theirs...

He had made his way to the elevator, waiting for the doors to open. When they did, an android stood, motioning for him to keep quiet. Aiden's confusion played on his face plainly. The android motioned to a dark room, zipping over to it. When the android twisted the door knob, it wouldn't budge.

"Locked," the robot murmured.

It twisted the knob harder this time, breaking the lock mechanism and ushering Aiden inside. Aiden followed without debate. When the door closed behind them, Aiden stared at the android in the dark, waiting to hear what it had to say.

"Please tell me I made the right choice in following you," Aiden said.

"Aiden, this unit is known as Pro Ten-Four. A problem has developed. Nemo and Bastion couldn't meet you at the rendezvous point because they've been captured by Cerberus and the androids doing its bidding," the robot said in its best synthesized whisper voice.

"I figured something had gone wrong," Aiden muttered, mostly to himself. "Are they okay? What happened?"

"It appears that their plan had been found out. The androids following Cerberus' orders captured them shortly after you parted."

"Do we know where they're being held captive?" Aiden asked, eager to arrive and rescue his friend.

"Yes, but you'll have to be careful. You are sure to have eyes watching you harder than ever before. Stealth will be key," the android replied. "We believe we've found a new way in; one they haven't found just yet."

"What about Larina? Have you guys found her down there in your searches? Can we still save her, too?" Aiden was hopeful now.

"It is possible," Pro said. "Assemble a team and meet this unit on the first floor near the elevator. Be discreet. We can't afford another ambush by Cerberus' programmed androids."

"Understood."

Aiden, Gord, and Hobbes exited the elevator, looking for the rebel android. They did their best to be inconspicuous, waiting for the robot they were supposed to meet. They didn't have to wait long though before Pro opened up a hidden door in the wall, motioning them to come forward.

The three men disappeared through the small door, following the android through the maze once inside. The hallways twisted and turned, confusing Aiden. If he were to try to figure out which way was North at this point, he'd be spinning around in circles.

"I'm wishing Deacon was here too," Hobbes said.

"We couldn't all just suddenly vanish," Aiden said. "Deacon will be the distraction if we need it."

They crouched as they sped through, listening for the android to speak and give them any kind of information, but it never spoke. After a while, Pro slowed, holding his arm out to stop the humans behind him.

"This is their main laboratory," the android explained. "Nemo could be here, but Bastion likely won't be. This unit hopes that they have not been moved here yet and that they're still in the holding cells. But here is where their mission is being carried out. See for yourself. As we pass through here, it is important that we are absolutely silent; they are sure to react if they become aware of something happening in their main lab."

The Stormwalkers nodded in understanding; it was clear that this place had an importance to Cerberus and its androids, and while they needed this information, they would have to be the more careful than ever since their arrival.

They tiptoed into the open space, focusing very hard on their steps. Aiden was trying to stay close to the android in front of him, and hadn't been looking around at the lab much. But when he heard a gasp come from Hobbes, he whipped his head around to catch what had frightened him.

Hobbes was looking at the far wall where there stood a flat platform, raised a few feet off the floor. Resting atop the plat-form was a large capsule, almost like a tub. There was a large computer station near the platform with cords that attached to this tub with lots of flashing lights and words scrolling on the screen. Hobbes stood at the tub's side, looking into its contents.

Aiden made eye contact with Pro, nodding his head to the vat. The android waited a moment before giving a single nod. Aiden thus changed his trajectory to move toward this new discovery. They moved slowly and quietly, and before long they were standing in front of this vat. He stepped onto the platform, so he could look into the tub and view what Hobbes had discovered.

By this time, Hobbes had clasped his hand to his mouth. He stepped down from the dais, looking away. Gord sighed, sadly, shaking his head. Aiden stared in amazement. Inside this vat was a weak and withered man. His body was submerged in the water that filled the tub-- Aiden couldn't even be sure if it was completely water, as there was a filmy, viscous nature to it. The man's body was wrinkled, his eyes very sunken with dark circles under his eyes, of which peeked out from above a long beard that would have been full and flowing if not for being soaked in the vat. The man looked like a bearded skeleton.

But the identity of the withered man is what struck Aiden the most. As the realization finally came over him, he slipped, barely catching himself at the edge of the tub.

"Is he alive?" Hobbes whispered from the first floor, still unable to look.

Aiden tried to watch the elder's chest to measure if it rose and fell with breath. It seemed to be, if only slightly. Aiden looked at Hobbes and nodded. Hobbes sighed, scared, knowing now they had to save him, too.

"I don't get it," Gord said. "'Yer real spooked, Aiden. You know that old guy or something?"

Hobbes glared at him.

But Aiden seemed to pay the remark no mind. "We gotta help him. Gord, this is my grandfather. This is Jonah."

CHAPTER EIGHTEEN

JONAH, Deacon's father-in-law and Aiden's Grandfather, was being tested on by these androids.

How the hell did he get here?

Aiden was floored. A part of him had expected to never see the Pathfinders again, Jonah included. He'd only just begun to reconcile with that idea, and now this?

How are you here, Jonah? And what have they done to you?

"Okay. This won't be easy," Aiden said. "The androids had their plan from the beginning. But this isn't over yet. Gord, I want you to take Jonah to safety. I want you to take him back as far as we had gotten when we first ran into Uka in the swamp. Go, and the rest of us will meet you with Nemo, Bastion, and Larina. I hope so, anyway. We'll meet you as soon as we can. Wait for us."

Gord nodded and went to help Jonah.

Hobbes looked at Aiden with determination in his eyes. "Look what they did to him. They planned to do the same to us? We gotta find Nemo and Larina before it's too late."

Aiden gave one nod to those who were left. "I have a feeling that they'll be well protected, so prepare to fight like hell."

There was a murmur among the group, but they all seemed satisfied. Soon, they were marching forward, further into the darkness.

Nemo jerked awake. She had been having a dream where she was falling, and her body suddenly snapped back into consciousness.

The sharp movement startled Bastion, who'd been keeping watch in the dark. "Bad dreams?"

"So you care about how others feel, now?" Nemo half joked.

Bastion looked off into the dark that surrounded them. "The things I've done, the things I believed. Sometimes I wonder if I ever had a heart."

Nemo winced at the remark. She'd meant to make a light jab, but had possibly opened another old wound in him. "I'm sorry. Of course you have one, Bastion. I'm sure there is something, someone, that you truly cared about?"

He was quiet for some time. She began to think he ignored her, when he simply stated "Yes."

Realization came to her. "What was her name?"

Bastion turned to her, the pistons in his back and neck hissing ever so lightly. She spotted the cybernetic eye looking her way in the dark. He held its scope on her.

"Mira."

"So the mighty Bastion had a girlfriend-"

"You know nothing of it!" Bastion growled. His robotic vocal box made his temper all the more ominous. "Do not belittle what memory I still hold."

She winced again. She had to remind herself who she was talking to. Bastion had been a zealous fanatic while an assistant to Jorus and the Eagles. What regret he still held for that time was only multiplied by his physical state now. He was a walking prison of his own self, and she felt saddened for it.

"You're right," she said. "I don't know your story, not the full story. But I'd like to hear it."

"You're just trying to be civil."

"No, I mean it. Really. Tell me about Mira."

Bastion regarded her a moment, and agreed. The former Eagle then told the Stormwalker the story of his life and Mira.

As Aiden and his team sped off, Gord and Pro went to work getting Jonah from the tub.

"Be very careful, friend Gord," Pro said. "We don't know how fragile Jonah is, or how far the experiments have gone with him. But we need to pull him out of this tub, and we will likely have to carry him out to safety. This unit believes Jonah will not be able to walk on his own."

They reached into the vat of water to help lift Jonah out. Gord half expected Jonah to start gasping or struggling the moment they pulled him pulled out of the water, but he stayed immobile. It wasn't long before he was entirely out of the tub, dripping water all over the platform and covering Gord and Pro as well. They laid him on the floor, checking his vitals.

"It appears he is still alive, if only just," Pro said. "Let us take him away from here."

Gord hoisted Jonah onto his own shoulders to carry the feeble man.

"We stay in the wall tunnels," Pro stated. "Then we'll be in the walls for most of the journey, and mostly invisible to the compound until reaching the front entrance. We may be able to escape without being noticed. Especially if the androids are guarding Nemo and Bastion, which this unit believes to be the case."

Gord nodded in agreement, as they began to make their way back towards the hole in the wall whence they came.

"Wait, what is that over there?" Pro pointed.

Gord's head turned to the darkest corner of the room. It was difficult to make out, but something moved, causing the sound of metal on metal scraping. Gord remained back with Jonah while Pro approached the unknown shape. As Pro got closer, he discovered another cell built into the dark wall, metal bars dividing the space between Pro and the person held within. Pro went to work on the cell door.

Gord steadied himself, shifting Jonah's weight on his shoulders. He couldn't quite make out what Pro was doing, until the sound of a snap of a lock being broken sounded. Then a moment later, the android returned carrying a bundle of a person in his arms. He saw chains on the person's wrists, and as Pro shifted the figure slightly, a familiar face revealed to him.

Gord's face lit up. "Larina!"

By the time Bastion had reached the end of his tale, Nemo was speechless. Her outlook of him, her memory of Bastion during their mission through the Storm, had changed dramatically.

They'd all been quick to the wrong conclusion of the young Eagle, she knew that now.

"I see you, Bastion," she said finally. "I see you."

He nodded. She figured he didn't quite believe her statement to be real, and that was alright. She would try to help him, over time. If they had the time, that is. She then realized they had been stuck for quite some time, in the dark, in the silence.

"How long do you think they're going to keep us in here?" Nemo asked, the terror lacing her voice. She cringed at the thought of what would come next after the androids returned for them.

"I do not know," he said. "Soon, they're going to come looking to use you too, like the others must be."

"What about you?" She worried about the answer.

He hesitated a moment before answering. "I am compromised now. The likely result would be termination."

"No way," Nemo said, standing. "They can't do that to you. They wouldn't terminate you. Why? Haven't you been a resource for them?"

"I was, yes. And I believe I was an...efficient tool, too. The blank spots are many. I'm not sure of everything that occurred during those times, but I have been useful to them. That very thought disgusts me. But I am no longer viable. I am grateful for the wake up, Nemo. I am. But I prefer termination over reprogramming no matter what."

Nemo stayed quiet for a long time. "The Stormwalkers will come for us. Don't you worry. We're going to help get you out of here. You're one of us, Bastion. Like old times."

"A nice thought," Bastion said, looking down at his hands. "But I learned long ago not to hold onto hope."

"You can't think like that," she said. "You have to think that this is all going to work. Trust them. And if you can't trust them, at least trust me." She took a few steps toward him, bending down to meet his eyes.

His human eye stared into hers. "I think I can do that," he said, barely audible.

Aiden moved quickly in pursuit of Nemo. The group darted through the hallways, looking for some kind of dungeon that Nemo and Bastion would be locked up in.

"Do we have any idea where they might be?" Hobbes asked.

"It'll be either near the labs, or somewhere within the central A.I. compound," Aiden replied. "They've gotta be."

"Well that's good news, at least," Hobbes murmured.

There was a loud bang of metal on metal. The sound startled the group, and they all flinched before getting into the ready position.

The muffled sound of voices appeared in the distance, and as he concentrated, Aiden heard Nemo's voice echoing around the damp halls.

"You're clumsy sometimes after all huh?" her singsong voice rang out, the laughter flowing easily from her throat.

"It's a tight space in here," Bastion's voice said back.

The sound of their banter raised Aiden's nerves. He knew they were together here, which was good, but hearing them like this was... not what he expected.

"Come on," he said, ready to dive in and save his friend from certain danger. But was she *really* in danger? Did she need him to swoop in?

He shook his head; of course she needed saving. She was

locked in a cage with Bastion, after all. Yes, the androids used him as well. But it was still Bastion; the annoying, self-entitled brat of an Eagle that had endangered their expedition multiple times. There was no getting out of that one.

"Nemo?" Aiden called out, perhaps louder than he should.

"Aiden?" her voice came back. She sounded confused, like she didn't expect for him to be there.

"We have to get out of here," Aiden's words were hurried as they broke the lock and pulled open the metal door. "They're sure to be on to us by now."

Nemo scrambled to exit the cage and Bastion followed close behind. The group turned back to sneak through the tunnels the same way they came, when a voice called out.

"Stop!" an android voice rang out. A small army of androids began to surround them.

"Run!" Aiden shouted, sprinting forward.

The androids were quick though, and soon the robots were right on their tail. The group was still a distance from the hole in the wall that would lead them to safety.

"Go!" Bastion declared. "I'll hold them off."

Nemo whipped her head around to look him in the eye. She sent an unspoken plea to not follow through with his plan, but then Aiden grabbed her hand, pulling her along. She felt her arm practically pull out of its socket, but she continued to resist.

"Go," Bastion whispered, but Nemo couldn't accept it.

He stopped running and let the androids descend upon him.

Nemo whispered "No," and she could not hold back the wave of pain that ripped through her. At the moment, she could not tell if the pain flared for herself, or for Bastion.

CHAPTER NINETEEN

Aiden sensed Nemo's shoulder pop out of place the moment it happened. He immediately let go of her hand, a sense of resentment toward himself for pulling so hard. He had wanted to save her so badly, but he instead hurt her. He then realized that from his actions, he was trying to save her from Bastion, rather than the androids themselves.

He felt like a monster.

Nemo sunk to her knees in pain. The sound was constant, and he couldn't glance at her without experiencing a sharp pain in his chest. He scrambled to his knees and crawled to her, doing his best to gather her in his arms and pull her to safety, but she would not budge.

Hobbes noticed that Aiden struggled to pull Nemo to safety, and sprinted to the two of them. He slid across the floor on his knees until he helped Nemo up on her other side.

The world then seemed to move in slow motion.

The androids swarmed around Bastion's limp body, pulling and tugging at his mechanical parts. They surrounded him like vultures, and Nemo couldn't do anything except watch as her unexpected friend that had sacrificed himself for her got over-whelmed.

She wouldn't walk. Her legs would not bend the proper way in order to carry her off to safety. Aiden and Hobbes lifted her by her arms, pulling her in the opposite direction, Aiden being careful of her newly injured shoulder. She dug her heels into the floor, slowing their progress.

"Nemo, we have to go," Aiden grunted through clenched teeth.

"If they catch us, it'll all be for nothing," Hobbes pointed out. "Don't let it be for nothing."

"Maybe we'll be able to come back for him," Aiden said. He had no real belief it would be possible, but he had to think of something to motivate her to move.

The androids dragged Bastion off to be used or destroyed, they had no idea.

"We'll come back for him," Hobbes echoed.

At that, Nemo's legs gave way. Instead of holding herself back, dragging her feet, she just let go.

"Nemo...?" Hobbes warned.

Several of the remaining robots zeroed in on Nemo as a weak link and easy target. These units made a beeline for the group of three, and Aiden and Hobbes quickly decided what their next move would be.

"Fight or run?" Hobbes asked.

"We're out of time, Hobbes," Aiden said as they backed away. "We gotta fight."

"I don't think she's got any fight left in her," Hobbes muttered.

Both men glanced at Nemo, now slumped to the ground, no longer supported by Hobbes or Aiden. Aiden bit his lip, not sure if he could fight them off and protect Nemo at the same time. He needed her to get herself up and moving.

"Nemo, I know you're upset, but now would be a great time to move..."

In an instant, Nemo appeared to gather up a surge of energy from an unknown source. She got to her feet, her eyes set and a determined expression on her face.

"Hobbes, I'm going to need you to pop my shoulder back in right now," she said, her voice stronger than it had been all night.

Hobbes wasted no time in rushing to her side. "One, two, three!"

He pulled her shoulder into place, hearing the pop when it returned its proper place. Nemo's face didn't even contort into a wince.

"So... a fight, then," she said.

Then she was off, running full tilt at the swarm of androids coming at them. Hobbes and Aiden looked at each other for a moment, confused about the violent switch that had just taken place. But there was no time to dwell; they charged after her, not sure how exactly they would take on all these enemies.

Aiden remembered a small detail he'd put aside prior to finding Nemo again. Reaching behind him, he pulled Nemo's staff from his belt. He gripped it in hand, extending the ends to their full length, and handed it to Nemo, who took it in surprise. She glanced at him, and a smirk replaced her surprise.

Nemo led the charge, and wielded the familiar weapon in her trained way, first spinning the staff in warning, and swinging it at any enemy that came within arm's reach. She was vicious and brutal, like Hobbes and Aiden had never seen.

The two men followed her lead and picked up their own scrap tools as weapons, and wielded them as best they could.

Soon, Aiden became consumed with each enemy that fell before him. He thought of nothing except swinging his weapon to inflict maximum damage upon each android that faced him. The robots fell one right after the other and Aiden sensed a feeling of invincibility wash over his body, like there was some unseen force that helped him take down these enemies one at a time, sometimes more.

He was so enveloped with his own fight that when he heard the scream, he hesitated before turning to see what had happened. When his head swiveled upon the scene, he froze. Something struck from behind, but not hard enough to knock him out. It pulled him back to the reality that he faced.

He swung his weapon upon the android, taking it down with one hit. And another, and another, his rage taking him over. He saw red and a yell ripped from his chest as he continually plowed through enemies.

There was a lull, for a moment, and Aiden viewed a straight shot to the hole in the wall. On the other side of the room, more robots spilled in, coming for the remaining Stormwalkers. He sprinted to the hole in the wall, faster than he believed his legs would carry him. In the span of a moment, Aiden found himself surrounded by damp dirt walls, safe from the androids for another few moments.

Nemo watched as Bastion's body was beaten and battered by the androids, and overwhelming defeat creeped into her very spirit. She knelt on the floor, resigned to that spot with no energy to move. She could vaguely understand Hobbes and Aiden going back and forth, debating what to do with her.

Their words were like knives stabbing her, in a way that she couldn't put into coherent thought. She sat there, doing everything she could to convince herself to raise off the floor and fight. It was only a matter of time before the enemy closed in on them; she needed to pull herself together.

She imagined her friends losing. She pictured what the androids would keep doing to them, and once finished, disposed of. They were nothing.

Brief hints of Aiden's voice echoed in her ears. The exact words were lost, but his intention came through. It took some time, but Nemo's resolve slowly regained its footing. Her determination managed a rebellious climb out of the darkness and back to the matter in front of her. She took a deep breath, standing. She set her jaw, determined to fight until they were safe. They would come up with a plan to save Bastion. It was not the time to fall apart. She wouldn't let another fall. Not another friend.

"Hobbes, I'm going to need you to pop my shoulder back in right now," she said, her voice suddenly a pillar of strength.

Hobbes was by her side in seconds. He grasped her arm, ready to shove it back into place. "One, two, three!"

He pushed her shoulder into place, and a pain rippled through her body. Though aware of the pain, she didn't let it slow her; she didn't even grimace.

She stood proud and tall, her jaw set and determined. She was going to take these androids down for what they had done to Bastion; for what they'd tried to do to all of them.

She took off, running at the army of robots, aware of her friends following after her lead and mimicking her movements to defeat the enemies that presented before them.

A flash of metal, and then her own staff was in her hands.

Gripping the staff, remembering its familiar shape and weight, she was ready. She swung it at an oncoming android, causing heavy damage. So she swung again and again until the robot fell, incapacitated. A sense of accomplishment and strength like she had never known emanated from within. Any robot that got in her way would be taken down.

She was aware of her friends fighting beside her, brandishing their own weapons and taking down each android that they came up against. She recognized their cries of victory, the celebrations as they knocked down another robot, then another. But she couldn't focus on their victories, as she had her own battles to wage. The androids were not slowing down, coming one after another.

She was so focused on her battles that she hadn't been paying much attention to anything else. And so, when the scream echoed out toward her, she whipped her head around in surprise to see what had happened.

When she saw the mess before her, she panicked. Her heartbeat stopped. She slashed at another android before running to her fallen friend.

Hobbes lay prone on the floor, a deep gash in his chest. Blood seeped through his shirt, and it spread like a running river. She knew it was stupid to abandon her focus to go to him. But Hobbes was one of her closest friends, and she would not leave him bleeding on the floor alone.

She looked up at Aiden, who now fought even harder; the waves of androids weren't slowing. Nemo turned back at Hobbes, who's eyes were wide as he stared at his chest. He was having a hard time keeping his head up to see where the blood was coming from.

"It's gonna be okay," Nemo said, her hands shaking and hovering over his abdomen. "It's gonna be okay."

"Nemo," Hobbes gasped and managed a smirk of blood-stained teeth. "You don't have to lie."

"No, no, you're going to be okay. We're going to get you out of here and you're going to be fine," she kept repeating.

"I think... I think this is where we say goodbye..."

"No," Nemo said, her voice strong. "I can't."

"Nemo, go. Get outta here..." his coughs came with painful spasms. "Try not... to miss me... too much..."

"Hobbes," she croaked.

Her eyes stung of thick tears. She wiped them clear with her sleeve, and realized Hobbes was gone. And although his eyes were hollow and void of life, his lips rested in a defiant smile. A joker to the last.

She looked up to the hole in the wall, seeing an opportunity for a straight shot. She knew she had to take it while she could. Without looking for Aiden, without another look at Hobbes, she sprinted to the hole, disappearing into the safety of the secret passage the rebels had constructed. She could hear Aiden's fast footsteps not far behind, but she didn't turn around to face him. She didn't know if she could look him in the eye. She had never felt more alone.

CHAPTER TWENTY

Gord waited in the hollow for Aiden and Hobbes. He had no idea if they were going to be able to find Nemo and Bastion and retrieve them, but he could only hope everything went according to plan. He paced back and forth, biting his thumbnail.

"How long does it take to go in on a rescue mission?!" He shouted into the hollow at nobody in particular.

"They'll be back, do not worry," Pro replied. The android busied itself with applying a damp cloth to Jonah's forehead. "There might have been complications. They'll show up."

The thought was not reassuring. Gord went back to gnawing on his thumbnail and pacing.

Some time later, Gord heard a shuffling noise which caught his attention. His head snapped up, and he immediately tensed, on guard. Whatever it was, Gord was ready to take it on and defend the Stormwalkers. When he realized what made the noise, however, he sprinted toward it.

Aiden stepped into the clearing with Nemo leaning on him for support. She looked like a zombie, hanging on to Aiden and following his every step. Gord swept in, offering his help.

"I'm glad y'all are back. We were getting kinda worried," he said to Aiden. "I didn't know if you guys were gonna make it back." His eyes flashed to Nemo.

Aiden gave him a look, making it clear there was more to say, but now wasn't the time. Maybe not as long as Nemo was there to hear. Whatever had happened must've affected her a ton.

"Give me a minute," Aiden muttered, taking the full weight of Nemo back on his shoulders and shuffling her somewhere comfortable.

Gord stood, waiting to learn exactly what happened. He swiveled his head around to take stock of his group when he noticed one face was missing...

Aiden shuffled back into the clearing to relay the mission to Gord. His arms were crossed, and his face showed defeat. He sighed heavily, ready to give a full report, but got cut off by Gord.

"Where's Hobbes?"

Aiden stared back at Gord, a sad look in his eyes, but he didn't reply.

"Aiden, where is Hobbes?" Gord asked again, more forcefully this time. His voice was not as steady, and he thought he would lose his temper.

Aiden sighed once again. "Things... didn't go as we'd hoped."

"Damn it, Aiden, what happened? Where is Hobbes?"

"He didn't make it, Gord," Aiden stated, his voice quavering.

"What. Happened."

Aiden launched into a retelling of their mission. He told Gord about the ambush, and how Bastion had sacrificed himself so the rest of them might escape. He told Gord he believed Bastion did what he did to save Nemo. He described how devastated Nemo was to witness Bastion being taken away, and how she suddenly gained the strength to fight. And then he told Gord that during the fight Hobbes had fallen, and Aiden missed it while he was battling androids of his own.

Gord bit his bottom lip and looked off to the side, angrily. He wanted to throw something, to feel something break. Hobbes was too pure to be the only one to not make it. He didn't deserve to go out that way. Gord had spent a lot of time with the guy and felt guilty he couldn't help him.

"How did this happen?" Gord asked, more to himself than to Aiden.

"We... we can't lose focus here," Aiden said, laying it on thick.

"What does that mean?"

"We were forced to run away; we were not prepared for that fight. It was a complete ambush and most of us got away when we could. But we need to go back. First, to get Bastion out of there, if we even can. Second, there are hundreds of androids in that building with no idea Cerberus is trying to make its own brand of humans. They aren't aware of the central A.I.'s leftover directives. They just do as Cerberus says. They don't deserve to be slaves to Cerberus and its closest androids. We need to spare those who are not a part of this whole thing."

"We're gonna go back for men who aren't even men?"

"They are beings with their own thoughts and goals, if they can be freed. We have to go in and help. That's what we do, remember?"

Gord rolled his eyes, clearly not agreeing with this plan.

"Hobbes is... Hobbes is gone," Aiden continued. "But there are others we can help. These people-"

"Robots."

"A lot of them don't have a say in what's happening. We can

help them. We can even help Bastion. If we run away now, then why ever leave Safe Harbor again? Why search for some survivors if we're going to ignore others?"

Gord was looking off in the distance, over to where he knew Nemo to be resting. He would not meet Aiden's eyes, but he did nod, knowing he was right. "Fine. So what's the plan?"

Aiden sighed for the hundredth time, but didn't answer right away.

"I'm not sure yet," he said, honestly. "I need some time to put something together. I don't want our group to go in and find ourselves ambushed yet again. I don't want to lose anyone else. I don't think I can take that."

"I don't think any of us can," Gord said.

"I know," Aiden said quietly. "I know."

"All I'm saying is the plan better be a solid one, because we can't take the morale of this group sinking any lower."

"We're not losing anyone else; I promise." Aiden claimed.

"You can't promise that, not if we're going back into that fire," Gord declared, stone faced.

"I'm promising it, anyway. I'm not letting anything else happen to us. We're all going to make it back to Safe Harbor. We're all getting out of here alive."

Gord sighed, rolling his eyes. "You better hope so."

Aiden sauntered back into the clearing where most of the Stormwalkers had fashioned sleeping arrangements. He spotted Deacon and made his way over to him, knowing he'd have to be the one to tell Deacon what had happened to Hobbes.

"It's good to see you," Deacon gave a halfhearted smile.

"You're not going to think so when I tell you what happened," Aiden said, rubbing the back of his neck.

"I haven't seen Hobbes. I assume you're going to answer that for me," Deacon said, wisely.

"Hobbes won't be coming back," Aiden said, as tears he fought so hard to hold back finally began to flow. "He didn't make it."

Deacon sighed deeply, closing his eyes. "Right. I'm so sorry, Aiden... What can I do?"

A moment and then, "I don't think it's quite hit me fully yet," Aiden wiped his face and took a seat on the ground next to Deacon. "Maybe I'm numb to it all..."

"Perhaps you understand you have a larger job to complete," Deacon offered. "Others are depending on you. Perhaps that is your priority right now."

"You should see Nemo; she's not well."

"I got a glimpse of her for a moment. She looked..."

"Far away?"

"Yes, I suppose that is an acceptable word for it. Losing Hobbes could have such an effect..."

It was like Deacon was reading his mind; as if he could travel right into Aiden's thoughts and observe what had happened. Aiden was reliving the last few hours, seeing Bastion running with the group, telling Nemo he was going to help her, and then just stopping. He could see the androids piling on Bastion like a wave of scavengers. He saw Hobbes laying on the ground, his eyes plastered open, vacant.

"No," Aiden answered. "We saved Nemo, but lost Bastion, which really seemed to set Nemo off. I think if she had been ready to fight or run from the get-go, Hobbes might still be alive. But I never said that out loud until now. I don't want her or anyone else to get it in their mind Nemo's the reason Hobbes is dead."

"And we truly don't know if that would change anything at all," Deacon said, as if that might ease Aiden's nerves.

"I think the only way to get Nemo back to herself is to go back for Bastion," Aiden laid out. "We need to help the enslaved androids, and that includes Bastion."

"You can't be certain that will bring Nemo back to her old self, but I do think that would be a good start. Two of us were lost today; at least if we can get back one of them, she might come back to us a little," Deacon agreed.

"So now I need to figure out a plan to send our friends back into the fire and save a bunch of androids. Nobody is going to be very happy about that."

"Except Nemo," Deacon said.

"Nemo can't go. In her state, it'd be too risky," Aiden retorted, putting his foot down.

"You think you're going to tell everyone we're going on another rescue mission, and that she's going to be okay with you telling her to stay put? Have you met Nemo?"

Aiden pondered, knowing Deacon was right. "What if we just don't tell her?"

"Aiden, you are our leader. This is your choice. Make the decision, and lead us. But just be very sure you're prepared for the fallout."

Aiden threw his hands up in the air, wondering how he was going to come up with a plan to keep them all alive while also pulling off this new mission. "This might be more difficult than I thought."

"Isn't it always?"

Nemo rolled over at the sound of Aiden's voice. He had not come to her area to visit her, he was instead visiting Deacon. He relayed what had happened back at Building 234, refreshing her memory and bringing back visions of Bastion and Hobbes she wished she could put away forever.

And then Aiden voiced what she had been fearing all along: that Hobbes had died because she was too distracted over losing Bastion. She closed her eyes and felt a hot tear run down her cheek. She would never be able to forgive herself for this.

She overheard Aiden suggest the Stormwalkers go back to save the androids, including Bastion, and her ears perked up. For the first time in hours, she had the energy and determination that she hadn't had since losing Bastion.

"Nemo can't go. In her state, it'd be too risky." Aiden's words cut like a knife. She was ready to march in and make a case for why she needed to be on the team that went back. The only way she could make up for getting Hobbes killed would be to save Bastion and the other androids. There was no other way to make up for it. If she was going to carry the guilt of killing Hobbes forever, she at least wanted a way to make something right.

Just as she readied herself to make her case, Aiden retreated back out to another area. She laid herself back down and began working on a speech to convince Aiden to let her go back. She would not be left behind.

CHAPTER TWENTY ONE

The next morning, Nemo searched for Aiden. She hadn't been able to turn her brain off all night, wondering how she would convince Aiden to let her go with them back to save everyone. She had pushed everything else from her thoughts while she worked on her speech.

But every once in a while, Hobbes' face swirled in her mind. The look that would forever be plastered on his features upon death. She shook her head to erase the image, but there a faint residue remained behind. She curled her upper lip, frustrated.

Nemo wandered around until she found Aiden. He spoke to Gord, presumably about the mission they would execute. She took a deep breath, squared her shoulders, and marched up to him with confidence.

"Aiden, can I talk to you for a moment?"

Aiden shared a nod with Gord, who stepped away, returning a knowing stare back at Aiden. Nemo watched as Gord went and spoke with the android Pro.

"How are you?" Aiden asked, gently. He placed a hand on her shoulder, looking at her with great concern.

This gesture, though kind and showing his concern for his friend, irritated her. She shook off his hand, rolling her shoulder up and around, a scowl etched on her face.

"I need you to stop treating me like I'm delicate--like I'm a glass toy that could break at any moment," she stated. "How long have you known me? How much have I gone through? Do you really think I'm going to fall apart?" She was insulted; she thought Aiden understood her better than that.

"Of course not. I'm just trying to help," he said softly.

"Would you treat Gord this way if he were in my position?" she interrupted.

"Yes, I would. Please don't turn this into something it isn't," he begged. "I'm just trying to do what is best for you."

"What is best for me is to go back with you as part of the mission," she crossed her arms over her chest.

"Nemo," Aiden groaned. "I really do not want to fight about this. The rest of us need to prepare, and I think it would be better if you stayed behind. This isn't what you want to deal with right now, but I don't think you're ready to go back."

His tone was firm, final. He sounded obviously exhausted. There was a tiredness to his voice that Nemo never noticed before.

"Aiden, you need the extra manpower. Your mission would be made easier with me there. I want to be helpful; it will take my mind off everything else. Please," she said, her eyes wide.

Aiden sighed, knowing full well it would be a losing battle to fight with her. Nemo's mind was made up, and she would not take no for an answer.

"You'd follow us anyway, wouldn't you?"

She nodded.

"Fine. We're leaving tonight. Be ready," he turned his back and walked away.

Though Nemo had won, she still felt a little defeated. She didn't like arguing with Aiden, or questioning his authority. It wasn't the proper way to deal with things, but she also had no real other choice here. She needed to convince him to let her go, even if that meant questioning his choices.

Nemo went back to gather her things and start planning their return with Aiden and the others.

Night fell unusually quickly. Before they knew it, they needed to make ready to trek back to Building 234 and begin their rescue mission. Nemo's target was Bastion; she would find and hopefully fix him, so she could have her friend back. She had gotten her hopes up he would be okay, and that she would be able to save him. After losing Hobbes, she just couldn't lose another friend to this madness.

They stood outside the building, and Aiden gave directions on how to sneak back in the same way they exited earlier. But Nemo didn't listen to Aiden, her focus solely on heading inside to find Bastion. She had a pretty good idea of where he might be, and mapped out the way in her head. As soon as Aiden gave the go-ahead, Nemo took off, booking it faster than she had ever run in her life.

She felt the air whipping past her face, seeing the dark, damp walls flashing by as she ran. She searched for the lab where the Stormwalkers found Jonah. If they were going to torture or reprogram Bastion, that would be the likely place to take him. He would need to be kept hidden away from the general population of other androids. That had to be the lab where Jonah had been kept. It was the most hidden away place they'd seen in the complex thus far.

Before long, she sprinted into the lab and her excitement mounted. This was it-- he would be here.

She spotted a work table with many cords tangled on top. She looked to see where the cords led, and saw in a makeshift chair sat Bastion. The cords from the table hooked up to him in a variety of places. She let her eyes follow the cords to the other end, and saw they were plugged into different computers, their screens flashing a mile a minute. It appeared Bastion was indeed being reprogrammed.

She tiptoed over to Bastion. She immediately spotted that the android workers seemed to have repurposed him. His mechanical parts had been rewired, reassembled, and generally placed back into a working order. His eyes were closed, but she could decipher the information from those computers being pumped into his mechanical self, and would soon infiltrate his brain. If Cerberus was programming him, they could only be pumping him with information that would make him an asset to their side. In a panic, she pulled the cords from him, hoping she wasn't too late. She grabbed him by the shoulders and shook him hard, as if waking him from a nightmare.

His eyes flew open, and he stared at Nemo, without a note of recognition in the light that shone out.

"Bastion? Bastion, are you okay?"

He tried to speak, but the words would not come to him. His human eye widened, and he looked terrified.

"Okay, it's okay. We're going to fix this," she started looking him over, wondering where she might even begin to fix him. "Come on, Nemo, you've got to remember something..."

She popped open his arm, looking at all the wires and little electric boards within. Her eyes sped back and forth, looking for something that might give her a clue. She realized there would be no sign telling her what would help, so she decided to take a chance. She pulled on a wire, yanking it out of its place, and Bastion started sputtering.

"Nope! That's not it," she said, her panic mounting. "We don't have time to sit in here and try things..."

She bit her lower lip, trying to decide what to do next. Could he run? How was she going to fix him? She had no clue what would bring him back to her.

"Bastion? Bastion, can you hear me?"

He nodded, his eyes still filled with fear.

"We're going to run. We have to find Aiden and the others. We're going to find the rest of the rebel androids and help them out of here. We're going to get all of you to safety, and we're not going out without a fight. But I'm going to need your help. I'm going to need you to run when I tell you to run, hide when I tell you to hide, and attack when I tell you to attack. Can you do that?"

Bastion nodded again.

"Can you tell me what I need to do to get you back in working order? I've never worked on anything like this before."

He shook his head no. He didn't know how to fix himself. Or if he did, it had been wiped out with the reprogramming.

This was not good news.

"Okay, we'll figure that out later. For now, let's just get the heck out of here," Nemo said. "We need to find Aiden and the others. We're going to meet up with them in the hole in your old hideout. Do you remember where that is?"

Bastion again shook his head no. Apparently, some of the

more important information had already been wiped out of his memory bank. Did he even remember who Nemo was?

"Bastion, do you know who I am?" She asked, her voice quavering.

There was a long pause before Bastion answered. His eye softened a little, and he nodded. He knew who she was; they didn't have the chance to wipe that out of his memory yet.

A weight lifted off her shoulders at his nod.

"Okay, let's go. Stick with me, and I'm going to run fast," she told him.

And they were off, sprinting through the lab and back toward the old rebel hideout where Nemo and Larina first reunited.

Bastion tried to keep up, but every once in a while, he'd slow down, caught up in bouts of spasms. Each time he would do so, Nemo's stomach would clench, worried about him.

"Once we find the Stormwalkers, we can take a closer look at what's causing this, but I don't want to leave us out in the open so exposed like this," she said, patting his human bicep.

Once he stopped shaking, they were up and running again.

Soon, they found the Stormwalkers and had Bastion sit down next to Aiden and Gord. She turned to her friends, worried. She explained the condition she found Bastion in, and how she pulled the plug during his reprogramming.

"He keeps shaking, and I'm not sure what's causing it. He doesn't remember some things, and he doesn't know how to fix himself, to put him back the way he was. I tried to fix him, but all I did was pull a wire, and he started sputtering like he was having a seizure. I don't know what to do."

Gord stepped in and squatted down, looking at Bastion's mechanical parts. He appeared to be taking stock of what Bastion was made of, taking notes in his head.

"I might be able to do something," Gord said after a few moments. "I need to sit down with him for a bit though. Do we have time for that?" His question was directed toward Aiden.

Aiden nodded, "We have to talk about our next move. Do what you can."

CHAPTER TWENTY TWO

The plans were made. Aiden's confidence over what would happen next began to grow. Fighting the general population of androids would cause collateral damage, but if they wanted to win this war, they'd have to take down the source, and that source was Cerberus.

Aiden started gnawing on his thumbnail, wondering if Bastion would be ready to join them. Gord worked on getting Bastion's cybernetic systems reset, but it had been slow going. Aiden worried about Nemo and her ability to balance her concern for Bastion in order to fight with the rest of the Stormwalkers.

He sighed and went to search for her. He found Nemo exactly where he anticipated she would be; sleeping next to Bastion's sleeping--does a cyborg sleep?--body. The picture was sweet, in a sense, but it pained Aiden to walk upon.

He debated whether he should wake her or not, but decided that she needed to be filled in. She needed to decide how she would proceed with the rest of the Stormwalkers. He nudged her elbow, and she snapped up almost immediately, as if she hadn't been asleep at all.

"What is it?" She asked, groggily.

"I wanted to inform you what our plans are, so you can decide what's next," Aiden replied.

Nemo nodded and stood up, stretching. Aiden led the way back to the sleeping quarters and sat down on one of the beds. Nemo followed suit, her face at attention.

"We're going to ambush them," he began. "At dawn. We're going for the central A.I., so we need to find our way to the underground area. We're going to have to take down android guards, I'm sure, but then we need to take Cerberus down. I need to know if you're going to be with us."

Nemo hesitated. She looked over at Bastion, who had not fully recovered yet. It was unclear if he'd recover at all from this ordeal. She was torn, and Aiden saw it plainly on her face. "You know that I want to fight with the Stormwalkers."

"We did kind of fight about it, yeah."

"But Bastion won't be ready by morning. We can't leave him here unprotected. What if something happens to him while we're gone? He won't be able to defend himself. We can't do that to him. He gave everything to help us in the past. I won't lose another friend. Not again."

Aiden didn't reply at first. He sat there, stoic, choosing his next words carefully. "I understand what you're saying, Nemo, but we could actually really use you during the ambush."

"This, after you didn't want me to go at all?" she asked.

"I was wrong," Aiden pointed out. "You're one of our best. We'll need you in there, fighting with us."

"Aiden, are you saying this just to keep my attention off Bastion?"

Aiden didn't have a good answer to that. He needed all hands on deck if they were going to take out Cerberus. They would be outnumbered, and the only real card they still held was the element of surprise. They couldn't spare any bodies to protect Bastion.

"I think that if you feel as though you need to stay with Bastion and be his protection, that's fine. Do what you have to," Aiden said. "I just need that decision now."

She stared at him for a moment. "Then I can tell you now that I will be staying behind with Bastion. If any androids come down here I'll take them out on my own."

Aiden hated the idea of her fighting anyone alone, but there was no arguing with her. She wanted to stay with Bastion, and there would be no convincing her otherwise. This was the path she chose.

"Nemo," he warned, trying to make it in a caring tone. "I don't like this."

"I know. And I understand why. But I need to be here. I can't leave him alone. I just can't."

"Nemo, it is not your fault that Hobbes is dead," Aiden told her, reaching out to grab her hand.

She drew it away. "Yes it is. Can't change that. But this is a way to do something about it. Please let me do this," she begged, her voice almost a whisper.

"Okay," he said, standing and straightening himself up. He withdrew his hand and walked away, wondering how this was going to play out for them.

The sun was going to rise any minute. Nemo's stomach tied in knots as she watched her friends pack themselves up and get ready to embark on their ambush. She wondered how many of them she would be seeing for the last time, but then forced those thoughts aside.

Aiden wandered himself over to say goodbye. He had an awkward half smile, plastered on his face as he approached. He tried to make light of the situation, hoping this wasn't the last time they would ever speak.

He reached Nemo, unsure of what he should say. Keep it light, in anticipation of seeing each other again? Or divulge his deepest and darkest thoughts as if this really was the end?

"So..." Nemo hesitated, as if reading, and sharing, his same thoughts.

"I hope this goes okay," he said.

"It will," she said. "You have to think it will, and it will."

"That there is some positive thinking," Aiden muttered, looking down at his hands.

"This isn't goodbye, Aiden," Nemo said, taking a step closer. She grabbed both of his hands in her own. "Please come back. I can't lose you, too."

I seem to be far from your thoughts lately. You just think of him. The thought flashed quickly, and faded again. He ignored it. "I wish you were coming with us," he looked up in her eyes as he said this, hoping she would change her mind.

"You know why I have to stay."

Aiden only nodded in response. He looked over his shoulder, realizing that the time to leave had come. When he turned back to glance at Nemo, he saw tears starting to well in her eyes. She nodded, repeatedly, unable to voice words.

"I'm not going to say goodbye," Nemo said, shoving him gently toward the exit.

"No goodbyes," he gave a halfhearted laugh. "See you."

He turned his back on Nemo and followed the rest of the Stormwalkers out of the hideout and began the trek to the central A.I.

Aiden felt the distance between himself and Nemo with every step he took. The regret at leaving her behind mounted. He sensed that something was wrong; he had never left her like this before. She was alone to protect herself and Bastion, and Aiden did not like it one bit.

"Stop worrying, Aiden," Gord said, snapping him back to reality. "We need you, here. Focus."

Aiden realized Gord to be absolutely right, and he did his best to put the thoughts of Nemo out of his mind. He did not want to put any lives in danger because of not being focused on the task at hand.

Before long, they stood outside the central A.I. platform, ready to attack. He was surprised at the lack of android personnel guarding the entrance, and knew they needed to be on alert as they entered. The moment they emerged into the A.I. center, the group cast their eyes on Cerberus itself.

The large machine took up the majority of the room. It's base was circular, tapering up to a raised dais which held its upper body, shaped in the approximate image of a person. The thing's head connected at the back to numerous cables and wires, which in turn led into rows of computers along the wall. Its arms and hands draped down and gripped the sides of the dais, giving the image of a partial woman on a throne.

So this is Cerberus, thought Aiden.

"What in the...?" Gord whispered.

"Okay, our goal is to destroy those computers," Aiden said. "We need to cut off the ability to communicate with the other androids. We cut those off, it has no resources left. Are we ready?"

A murmuring of both yes and no passed among them, both human and android, and yet they knew the moment had come; there was no going back.

They were off, sneaking through the open room that Nemo had once been locked up inside. Aiden's mind was stuck on that fact for longer than he should have been. He shook his head, pushing it out of his mind. He couldn't be stuck on Nemo. How many times did he have to remind himself of this?

But before anyone could reach Cerberus, controlled androids began piling in from all sides, clearly tasked with one singular order: to kill.

"Alright then," Aiden said as he pulled his pistol. "We fight!"

And then the rage of it all blinded him. He fired again and again, aiming for the androids' heads every time, androids falling over and crumpling into piles around the room.

He had tunnel vision, and could only focus on what lay directly in front of him. He could not think about his friends who were with him in this battle to the death, and he could not wonder if they had fallen prey to these awful steel beings feigning human life all around him. The thought of what they had done and what they were planning to do incited his rage. He thought of them kidnapping Jonah, using him as a guinea pig. He thought of how they lied to the Stormwalkers, making them lab rats under the guise of healing them. Of how Nemo had been captured, locked in a cage. He thought of her time alone with Bastion--and though he promised himself he wouldn't dwell on it, it fueled his rage.

As he shot down another robot, he let out a guttural yell. "WHY?!"

Of course, there was no reply. Instead, more androids descended upon him, several at a time. He heard a cry from one of his Stormwalkers, but didn't have time to look, as the androids surrounded him, like predators swarming their prey. For a moment, he thought he had been defeated.

Instead, he reloaded and used his momentum to swing and fire at another. The rest of the group fought on as well, but the numbers did not cease. They continued to emerge in waves, and Aiden began to see this to be a lost cause.

Just as these dark thoughts wormed their way into his mind, a sparkle of steel appeared in his peripherals. More androids had started to filter in, but when he took a moment to look, he realized these androids attacked the first group of androids. Android-on-android fighting filled the room, and Aiden realized the remaining rebels had joined the fray. To Aiden, the numbers suddenly seemed a lot more feasible that the Stormwalkers could prevail this day.

This gave Aiden hope; he was reinvigorated and had more life in his fight. He struck the robots down two at a time, three at a time. Aiden stood steps away from reaching the computers that connected Cerberus. He glanced up at the tall, imposing figure of the A.I. supercomputer, an unmoving figure of ancient creation that was responsible for all this chaos. As he stared, his fear grew when Cerberus' bald head turned, every so slightly, to bear her eyes down upon him. Her appearance was stoic, but was most definitely present.

She was aware.

He felt like this was his moment, that the time had come. He checked his pistol, and drew to bear on the critical systems of the computers.

And then he heard a yell of pain, nearly identical to the one from Hobbes before his end.

It sounded like death, and this time it came from Gord.

CHAPTER TWENTY THREE

They had sneaked through the underground tunnels, which the rebel androids reassured them repeatedly to be a safe route from the overseeing eye of Cerberus. Gord's heart raced with each footstep, pushing them closer and closer to the central A.I. area. Once they arrived, they would be in for a hell of a battle.

He glanced over at Aiden, who appeared distracted. It was written all over his face; he worried about leaving Nemo behind with Bastion. Anyone who knew Aiden also acknowledged his feelings for her, and leaving her behind likely ate him up inside. Gord understood the concern, but he if Aiden remained this distracted, they were not going to have a winning battle in front of them.

"Stop worrying, Aiden," he muttered. "We need you, here. Focus."

Soon they stopped outside the central A.I. platform, ready to launch their attack. Gord gazed around, his eyes fixated on what he assumed to be the computer known as Cerberus, taking a look at it for the first time. "What in the...?" He whispered. He started to worry at the sight, wondering exactly how the few of them were going to take this thing out, especially once the androids started to fight back. He didn't know how many androids were housed in this building, but he knew there were hundreds more of them than the Stormwalkers, and the fight would not be easy.

"Okay, our goal is to destroy those computers," Aiden said. "We need to cut off the ability to communicate with the other androids. We cut those off, it has no resources left. Are we ready?"

A murmuring of hesitation passed among them, but regardless, the moment was at hand. There was no other choice but to move forward and fight for their lives. Gord took a deep breath, hoping he would live to see more.

They took off, sleuthing through the wide open space, trying to find a place to hide and attack. There weren't a lot of places for them to hide for cover, a fact that didn't escape Gord's attention. He tried not to panic as he pondered where he would plant himself. He needed a plan and time to think, but he couldn't do that out in the open, for risk of being attacked unprotected.

Gord whipped his head around as the sound of androids pouring in through entryways took over any other thoughts. Nobody had yet reached the computers connected to Cerberus, and now it seemed they might never actually reach those systems. The androids came in waves, over and over, and panic settled into his stomach. He did not have a good feeling about this; almost like a premonition of what was to come. It didn't seem right, and he didn't think they had the ability to take on all of these robots. Suddenly the room filled with synthetic bodies, and Gord barely saw the Stormwalkers amidst the androids. The androids began their attack, each move with deadly precision.

Firing off his twin revolvers, Gord started to think none of them would make it out alive after all. He spotted out of the corner of his eye that Aiden had pulled out his pistol, firing with wild abandon.

An android approached him, ready to strike. Gord dodged the swing and shot the android in the head. The shell of its skull exploded like a shattered bowl. The next android came at him, and he fired his other revolver, stopping the robot cold. More and more came, and Gord could only rail off shot after shot, until ammo depleted.

With the other Stormwalkers fighting under similar conditions, he soon noticed piles of broken bodies littering the floor. It made movement more difficult, and he continued to estimate whether the number of attacking enemies dwindled at all.

He heard another body hit the floor and a painful shout into the void-- Aiden's. "WHY?!"

There was no time to ponder what Aiden referred to. Instead, a glint of movement flashed as more androids began to file in through the doorways. More robots than before, filing in multiples at a time. He spun around, and found they were surrounded on all sides by these things. How were they going to get themselves out of this one?

Behind him, an android swung at his knees, knocking him to the ground. He let out a cry of pain and surprise, but quickly picked himself back up, swinging his revolver and cracking it on the android's head. The strength of his strike managed to pop the android's head clean off. The panic set in again as he stared around at all the metallic forms. He no longer spotted Aiden or anyone else on their side. He continued to swing at anything that came close to him, not worrying about if they were friend or foe.

Another influx of androids piled in then, and Gord started to think the plan failed. How would they go out, then? Killed? Experimented on, tortured to death? But when he looked closer, Gord realized a remaining contingent of the rebel androids had appeared, coming to help in the battle. Gord's panic dissipated, instead reinvigorated with a sense of purpose and determination. They could do this. They had a chance.

With more allies fighting for them, Gord had more chance to take stick of the progress they made against the androids protecting Cerberus. He was almost giddy with excitement, as he swung at heads. It was like he simply skipped along, knocking androids down with each joyful swing. He was so focused on the good fortune of the rebel androids coming to fight, that he lapsed in paying close enough attention to his enemies. On a trajectory towards the computers which supplied Cerberus with its information, a gleeful smile on his face, a splitting pain ripped through his abdomen.

He stared down and found a bloodied android arm piercing through him from behind. The robotic fist punched its way right through his torso. The pain escaped his body as a cry into the void. The android withdrew its appendage, and Gord dropped to his knees, unable to hold himself up any longer.

The android stared at him a moment. Gord stared right back at that cold ceramic face. Then, without a word, his killer scurried off to launch an attack against Deacon. Gord wished he could shout a word of warning, but as he tried to move his mouth, the words would not escape his lips. He lifted his hands to touch the hole now showing squarely in the middle of his stomach.

Since joining the group and becoming a new Stormwalker, he thought dying would be an honor. Dying in battle was always a possibility, but protecting your friends and what you believe in made it worth it. He always believed that when his time came, he would die without fear, welcoming the darkness, but he didn't feel quite that way at this moment. At this moment, there was a strong sense of fear. The fear was very real.

His eyes darted around the room, looking for a familiar face. All he met was the synthetic bodies that piled up around the room, and the moving legs of the androids still attacking. Would his fall go unnoticed? Would he be forgotten?

He tried to take deep breaths, but the panic made it impossible. He just wished someone would come and sit with him, hold his hand, and tell him it was all going to be okay. Was this what Hobbes had felt in his final moments?

A tear escaped his eye as his consciousness faded. Gord then died, alone on the station floor.

Aiden whipped his head around, looking for Gord. His fellow Stormwalker's cry had rung out, but now he couldn't find him amidst the chaos of attacking synthetic bodies. He didn't have time to start the search, as the androids still flowed fast and hard at him. He only hoped he was wrong about the sound of his cry, and that Gord would be okay.

When he got the chance to look around again, he measured that their numbers had again decreased. He counted piles and piles of rebel androids as well, which caused a sense of fear to start creeping into his stomach.

And then Aiden spotted Gord, laying on the floor.

Little time remained, but Aiden ran to his friend, ready to grab him and carry him over his shoulder to safety. But when he arrived upon Gord's prone form, he saw the glassy stare of death in Gord's eyes, and he moaned in frustration.

He had failed another Stormwalker. He let another one die on his watch, and this time, Gord had died with little fanfare. Since becoming the leader of the group, he never felt like such a failure as right now. He screamed, ready to destroy any other android that got in his way. He was ready to rip apart anything and everything to rid himself of the anger and rage that built in his chest.

No one else had even realized Gord was not among them, which frustrated Aiden even further. How did they not notice one of their own was gone? He stayed silent, hoping when they reached Nemo and Bastion they'd still be there, safe and sound, so this could all be worth something.

He didn't think he could bear it if they never found Nemo. What would he do if Nemo had been hurt--or worse, killed--because of this? How many more Stormwalkers was he willing to lose because of his plans?

Their retreat was hidden by traversing the tunnels behind the walls, and Aiden reflected upon their luck over the way these routes had not yet been discovered by the android population. Why was Cerberus unaware of such a vulnerable point? He decided it just proved the ingenuity of the rebels, was thankful for it.

Upon their return, they found Nemo and Bastion ready and waiting for their allies to arrive. Nemo's face lit up when she watched the team traipse back into the hideout.

Aiden looked around at the team remaining. Only one android managed to make it back to the hideout with them. The android was one he recognized, but he couldn't remember the name. Tal, perhaps. Or Pro. The shock began to set in, and the overbearing weight of needed rest for a few hours settled in, before starting up with a new plan.

"I don't care how long it takes, or what we have to do. We will take down Cerberus. Mark my words, we are not leaving until this is over."

CHAPTER TWENTY FOUR

Nemo watched as her friends exited the hideout for the battle to come. She thought of this mission as--though necessary--foolish. She knew the numbers and the probability of the Stormwalkers coming out on top, and that they weren't good. Their group had dwindled, and Cerberus likely still had many slave units at its disposal .

She looked over at Bastion who appeared to be sleeping. Being a cyborg, did that mean he was more in a standby mode or something? Gord had done his best to get Bastion restored back to his previous state, so he'd have all his knowledge back. But that task was never completed before the group needed to leave, and so Nemo didn't know Bastion's state. Time would tell before Bastion woke and revealed all.

To the Stormwalkers and the rebel androids, Bastion would be the most useful as a source for information. As a tool for Cerberus, he likely held secrets the androids could use to secure their freedom, especially if this last assault didn't prevail. But for Nemo, it was an entirely different story. She shared a cell with him. She had learned how wrong they'd been about the young

Eagle, and she was determined he deserved as much of a chance as the rest of them. She was also very aware it to be a notion that Aiden would never be able to understand.

She wondered when exactly the disconnect began to form between her and Aiden. Was it as soon as she'd been taken hostage? Was it this horrific ordeal she had gone through that Aiden wasn't able to understand? He was the leader and voice of reason for the Stormwalkers. Even when the best possible solution was an unpopular one. Being the Stormwalkers' leader, and making the decisions that came with the role, drove a sort of rift between the two. And when Nemo was taken, it only widened the gap.

She wondered if Aiden would've abandoned the search for her if she never found him. Would she be as disposable as Larina? Would they have stopped looking for her if it'd interfered with returning to Safe Harbor? She added that question to the growing list of reasons she had been pulling away from her longtime friend.

She took a few steps to close the gap between her and Bastion, watching him. His eyes were closed, but she could see the organic one moving rapidly underneath his eyelid as if he dreamed intensely. She said a silent prayer for what seemed like the hundredth time that night, wishing Bastion's reprogramming would be successful.

She laid her hand on his metal arm, cool to the touch. Although offline, he held a recoil of fear from others. Understandable, but she hated it; he seemed to shudder at her touch, if unconsciously. The thought of that being true saddened her. She withdrew her hand and sighed.

She tried to imagine what the battle was going to be like. Would they all die? Would any return? What would she do if that happened, if it were just her and Bastion now? Would she be able to escape with Bastion at her side?

A vision of Bastion swam before her eyes; his two halves torn apart, mechanical and biological. His torso lay discarded, arms and legs missing. His chest no longer rose and fell; dead. Like Hobbes.

Then she turned the vision to herself, and what might happen to her. She saw herself replacing Jonah in the labs. She pictured herself laying in a vat of some strange liquid, turning her skin wan and lucid. She was alive, but barely, clinging to life by a thread. She imagined herself to appear very much like Jonah; inches from death, but saved by the androids that would keep her alive for the mere use of her DNA. Just a resource. Nothing else.

These thoughts did nothing to calm her nerves. She shuddered, hoping beyond hope the Stormwalkers would somehow pull through this, and they could all escape to return home. The idea of home was so hard to imagine now. They had begun this journey such a long time ago, with so many obstacles along the way. She wondered if maybe they were never meant to ever return at all.

Flashes.

Faces. The pallid visage of innumerable android beings, always tinkering, always changing what he was. A new piece here, take a part away there. He was a puzzle, and they were keen to solve him.

They speak of their orders. Generations pass, and still they adhere to their directive. They collect. They study. They alter. They report. But for all this time? Why? And to whom?

They speak of their masters. There is a reverence there. They act as if their creators were still present, or that they may one day return. But that's impossible. Even he, in his current state, knows the Stormmakers are long gone. They caused the Storms. They made this world. They made these synthetic people, and abandoned them. That was just the way it was. But how to get them to realize? And why must he be the one to pay?

He sees his arm, its cold metallic surface gleaming in the near darkness. The porcelain skin of the androids is a stark contrast to the blue steel of his cybernetic parts. It reminds him he is not one of them. But it reminds him he is no longer a man, either. He is neither. He is... other.

Rage builds within him. They have not taken that from him, at least. He will use it, and use it well. With a sharp twist of the metal arm his restraints are easily broken. He leaps from the table, the androids shout and scatter, and he begins his revenge.

Despite their cries, he is vicious and thorough. Soon, pallid synthetic bodies litter the laboratory floor. They whimper their disdain, but he does not care. He relishes whatever form of pain they hold.

Next, the wall. His metal arm crashes into the cracked surface again and again, the surface giving way with every strike. He laughs at his impending freedom, but the blaring sound behind him stops his caring. He spins, facing a second audible slam of deep, guttural sound. It is as if the heavens themselves have opened up, and a great horn sounds down directly upon the room. It drowns out the sensors in his synthetic ear, and his organic ear almost goes deaf. He staggers, but steadies and stares at the source of the sound.

A bright light glares at him. Massive machines he cannot recognize churn their way through ground and stone, and he realizes he is no longer in the lab. He now stands on a cliff, staring down at the objects in the distance. They bear down upon him, and they are not alone. Figures follow at their side, and in their wake. Their details are obscured, but they stride with purpose. They control the machines. They are the makers.

The Stormmakers.

They are coming.

Bastion began to stir, and Nemo's head snapped to him. His eyes twitched open, like a newborn waking from a nap. He reached his hand up to rub his human eye, gently. He shook his head for a moment, as if to clear the sleep from his mind, and pushed himself onto his feet. He now stood, looking around the room, gathering his surroundings.

Nemo stood stock still, like prey waiting for the predator to notice or to walk away. She held her breath, looking for any recognition in his eyes. As his eyes swept across the room, they stopped upon noticing Nemo. She kneaded her hands together, her nerves taking over her body. She waited to see if he would recognize her, or if it would be the same blank stare he had been giving her since she had found him.

"Bastion...?" she finally allowed herself to ask.

Time passed as if hours between the time she asked the question and his answer, until his face broke into a smile.

"Nemo. It's me," he said.

Relief filled her, then. *Good. Something to consider a success this day.* She grinned.

"How did you do this?" he asked. "How did you bring me back?"

Nemo sat down and explained how she had found him, how she pulled the plug on him during his connection to Cerberus, and how Gord had attempted a reboot of his systems.

"I believed you would do it," he said, nodding. "I mean, I guess I didn't really know. But when they had me, I knew I would find myself again, with your help."

"That is a lot of faith you put in me," she laughed, as if they were having a normal conversation about the weather. It was amazing how light she felt, now he was awake and back to normal.

"I do. I have to; you're more a savior to me than the Eagles ever were," he replied. "Where is everyone?"

The two of them looked around the empty hideout, and suddenly the truth of the situation came crashing down around Nemo all at once. She took a deep breath before she brought Bastion up to speed. With each sentence, his brow furrowed deeper. He was distressed by this mission. He couldn't stop being worried about the Stormwalkers and rebel androids as well.

"Do you think they'll be alright?" he asked.

"I really hope so," Nemo whispered back.

"Why didn't you go with them?" he questioned.

At first, she did not want to answer. It was awkward now, explaining the need to stay behind to protect him when he was up and well, fully capable of defending himself from anything that came through the door. It would be hard to describe the fear she had of him not waking up as himself. How to explain her worry and hope for him that she held?

So she tried, to the best of her ability. She told him how everything had told her she needed to watch over him, to protect him until he was himself again. She did her best to reiterate the conversation she had had with Aiden for him, when she explained to him she could not go with the Stormwalkers. She had to stay behind take care of him, defend him, if necessary. When she was finished, he stood quiet.

"Say something, please," she begged.

"You felt the need to stay behind with me instead of with your friends who you've known for so long. Your loyalties have changed. I'm not a Stormwalker. What of your friends?"

"I can't tell you why. I don't understand it, myself. I just know our group is so focused on helping the android city and returning to Safe Harbor that nothing else matters. Not even keeping us together. And when I was locked up--I know they searched for me, but if they never found me they would have eventually stopped. Lately, that hasn't sat well with me. If you and the rebels hadn't come to save me, I would be another experiment, like Jonah. And the thought of my closest friends leaving me behind like that... it's kind of where I've landed now."

Bastion nodded. "It is complicated. You had the need to protect my well-being. A need that surpassed helping your friends. And you can't explain why that need was there."

She nodded. "Yeah. Complicated."

"Perhaps not as complicated as you think." Bastion went serious. "While I was shut down, I saw things."

"What do you mean?"

Bastion pondered a moment. "I believe you needed to protect me for a reason. That reason is something I have seen in the androids' archived memory files. Something big."

This confused Nemo. She began to ask for clarity, when moments later, she heard shouts and stumbles as the Stormwalkers and an android came spilling in the entryway. The ruckus drew Nemo's attention from Bastion, as Nemo was happy they were back; this meant they had won, surely? Nemo and Bastion stood quickly to greet them.

When Aiden piled in, he looked disheveled and like he wore the weight of the world on his shoulders. He met Nemo's eyes and made a beeline for her, but the look in his eye told her he was doing it out of obligation and not the desire to see her. A stab of pain in her heart reeled at his look.

"Nemo," Aiden grunted. "We lost Gord."

It was so matter-of-fact, so clinical, she wanted to slap him. She couldn't believe he would let Gord die, but that he would also tell her in such a brutal way. It was so unlike him to speak to her in such a manner; she detested him for it, even if just for a moment.

She didn't respond to his statement. Instead, she turned her back on him.

Bastion's eyes met Aiden's across the room, and he could feel the resentment burning into him.

CHAPTER TWENTY FIVE

Aiden's shoulders hunched as he trudged back to the hideout to find Nemo and Bastion. He didn't look forward to giving her more bad news, but there would be no avoiding it. Due to being in and out of his thoughts, the trek back to the hideout was much shorter than the trek to the central A.I., and he suddenly faced the entrance to their hiding area.

He looked up to see Nemo and Bastion talking, and a dark cloud overtook him. How dare they sit together when Gord lay dead in the other room? How dare they be that way when Gord died scared and alone? Was this why she wanted to stay behind? So they could sit and gossip like little girls?

He shouldn't, but he let his frustration take hold of him. He knew he needed to keep a collected head, but instead, he marched forward, ready to confront Nemo with what happened, because that would be exactly what she deserved to know.

"Nemo, we lost Gord," he stated, bluntly.

The way he said it, as soon as he said it, he regretted his words. The anger evaporated out of his body when he saw her reaction. She looked at him as though he'd slapped her right in the face. His words hurt her, it was plain as day. Of course, she was upset at the loss of Gord, but it reached much further than that. He couldn't read her mind, and she certainly wouldn't let him in now.

She turned her back on him. She'd ignored him and his harsh reality. She had fled from Aiden himself.

He whipped around, stomping back to the sleeping quarters, needing to cool off before they figured out their next move. He had the shakes, and he a blockage welled in his chest. He wanted to scream, to punch something, someone; Bastion would do. Was Bastion stealing Nemo away from Aiden? But Aiden knew she wasn't a thing to be stolen, so why be so angry?

What was wrong with him? He sat for some time, trying to calm down. He took deep breaths, and began to rock back and forth, his eyes closed. He couldn't speak to anyone until he got over this thing. Why did something so minor affect him so greatly?

He laid himself down on his bed. He kept his eyes closed, trying to push all thought from his head, but visions of Hobbes and Gord kept swimming into his thoughts. He kept seeing their faces after death, scared and alone. They weren't ready to go, and Hobbes had so much life left to live. It was heartbreaking. Then Aiden realized, for the first time in a while, he was alone. Aiden felt a tear slide down the side of his face, and he allowed himself to make the most of this time.

Aiden cried.

Time passed. He wiped tears away as he heard footsteps approaching. When he turned his head to see who entered, he was shocked to find Nemo. She stood before him, meek and shy looking. It was a look Aiden never saw on Nemo before, and it baffled him. He felt like he was looking at someone else, someone he didn't even know. The two stared at each other, but didn't speak; words seemed to escape them both.

After what seemed like hours, but only just moments, Nemo broke the silence. "What's our next move?"

Aiden sat up in his bed, not expecting to talk strategy. He didn't know if he could yet. Ever since they first lost Nemo, Aiden had been thinking strategy. He forced himself to keep thinking about the next step, the next step, the next step. He was tired. He couldn't think about how they would get out of Building 234, out of the city, back through the swamps, and back home. He barely had time to ponder over Hobbes and Gord. He couldn't process the fact the androids captured and experimented on his grandfather. He couldn't understand how or why his grandfather even got here. There were so many things floating around in Aiden's head he wished he could sit with, but there was no time for that. He needed to lead, instead. He had to come up with the plans, the reason for doing anything, and do whatever he could to better ensure their victory. It was incredibly exhausting, and he didn't know if he could fight any longer.

He looked up at Nemo and met her eyes. She was ready, her face set and her eyes hardened. She held an anger for these androids, for killing her friends, for locking her up, for experimenting on them. Regardless of their lack of control, the androids had delivered so much pain on the Stormwalkers.

"I don't know," he replied, his voice ready to break. "We were so outnumbered. There was a moment when I thought we were all going to die, but then the rebel androids came in to help. They piled in and I thought we would get to Cerberus, but we just couldn't. And now, the rebel androids have been decimated, we've lost Gord and Hobbes, and I can't see a way for us to win this. Everything we've been through, this might be the end."

He was serious. Every time they'd gone to battle, someone had been lost, and he couldn't bear to lose anymore. What if it were Larina next time? Or Deacon? Or Nemo... He couldn't stand to lose her in the midst of everything else going on, intentions aside.

"I don't know how we're going to pull this off," he said, putting his head in his hands. "It looks hopeless."

"It can't be hopeless," Nemo said, determined. "Because that means Hobbes and Gord died for nothing. And I will not let their deaths be in vain, Aiden. I won't."

Aiden's frustrations began to grow again. He could feel it rising in his chest.

"Well that's great, Nemo. Then you go ahead and go in there, guns blazing, and let me know how that works out for you," he spat at her. "You didn't see when Gord died. You had to stay here instead. It was so important for you to stay behind with Bastion, you couldn't be there when Gord died, so it's interesting you're being so very high and mighty about avenging his death."

"Don't you dare. Don't you dare blame me for not being there. We talked about why I needed to stay behind, and we agreed. If you didn't like it, why didn't you say so? It's your job. You lead us," she shouted back at him.

"Oh, please. Like you ever take an order well," he laughed. "Nemo, I could have given you an order to come with us, but you would never follow through."

"Why are you being so mean? What's wrong with you?" She looked at him like he had four eyes.

"What's wrong with me? Our numbers are dwindling each time we run into battle. My grandfather was being experimented on by Cerberus for who knows how long, and I have no idea how he even got here. Not since the Stormwalker trials have we faced such chaos. I'm out of ideas to win this stupid battle, I'm afraid we're never going to find our way back to Safe Harbor, and you're pulling away from me. It's like I don't even know you anymore."

Nemo stayed silent for a few moments, taking in everything he said. After a moment, she answered, "You *don't* really know me anymore."

Aiden looked at her in shock, shaking his head back and forth. He put his hands out to his side and looked up.

"Aiden," she continued. "We've committed ourselves to helping people in the different eyes of the Storms. It's what we do. It's what we agreed on. There've been times when we were willing to do whatever it took for the sake of the mission, to make sure those who needed help got it. We've sacrificed our own people in that mission. And we were okay with that. But I'm not, not anymore. I've tried to explain that. Tried to show it. But you continue ever onward in the mission. You might have had to leave me and Larina behind, and I get it. I know you have to do what's best for everyone. I understand it, but I don't like it. It doesn't sit well with me anymore. I realize now I'm not okay with the Stormwalker mission anymore. There has to be more to it than just running in and rescuing others, always at the expense of ourselves until there's nothing left. I see that now. But you're different. You've been pulling away, and so have I. Your priority is the mission. You trained for this. My priority, I think, is simply to get a life back. But we can't let that come between us right now. Right now, we have to focus on what's happening right in front of us, which is getting the hell out of here and back to Safe Harbor. Stop being so negative and put your leader cap back on. Please. We've got to do this. After, if there is an after, we can figure out what life is all about, okay?"

Aiden hated every word that came out of her mouth, but she was right. He knew his priorities had to be in one place, and he had let some of them slide. They needed to figure out what their next steps were going to be. It was his job to do this, and he needed to be ready to come up with a plan.

"Fine," he said, firmly. "But we are going to talk about this when everything is said and done. Agreed?"

"Agreed," Nemo said, after taking a deep sigh.

"Now come help me, because I need new ideas. Clearly mine are not going as well as expected," Aiden conceded.

"Well, you're in luck because I always tend to have amazingly great ideas," she said, a more gleeful tone in her voice.

Aiden remarked she sounded a lot like how Nemo used to be, and it was comforting to see she hadn't totally disappeared in the time they had gone through all this. He hoped by the time they exited this place they wouldn't all be completely marked and changed by their time here. If it did, he knew it would stain his heart forever, as the place where he lost two of his closest friends.

"What do you think? What can we accomplish with just the five of us?" He asked.

"Six," she corrected. "Bastion."

"Right. You're right. Bastion makes six."

"Well..." And she began to craft a plan. As she spoke, Aiden's mind began to follow her line of thinking. It would be difficult, and they could not really anticipate how the androids would react or respond, but based on what they had seen so far, they had a pretty good idea of what they might do. It was possible Nemo's plan could work. Possible they could make it out of here alive. Aiden felt reinvigorated to go back out and fight.

"Okay, let's do this," he said, standing.

"Absolutely not! You need rest! You can't go right back in there!"

"They'll never expect us to attack right after we backed off. They would be vulnerable!"

"Aiden, think about what you just said. They're robots! They don't need rest!"

"Miss Nemo is correct," the final rebel android, which turned out to be Pro, approached. "They are programmed to destroy any approaching outsider. It doesn't matter when, they will take us out. They are primed and waiting."

"Don't think of them like people," Nemo said, and looked at Pro. "No offense."

Pro only blinked.

"Fine," Aiden said, sitting back down, sulking. He crossed his arms, pouting like a child. "Then when?"

"You're going to get some sleep, and then we'll plan when to go. Lay down and try to rest. Bastion and I will talk strategy until you wake."

Aiden hated they were going to do his job while he slept, but he did need the rest. He agreed, turned to the corner of the room, and fell asleep before he had another moment to think.

CHAPTER TWENTY SIX

Nemo lay awake in her bed, listening to the sounds of Aiden and Bastion breathing in tandem around her. It baffled her how they could be sleeping when their last chance to take down Cerberus rapidly approached. In a few hours time, they would be marching into battle yet again, this time the two people she felt closest to by her side, and the possibility any of them could be taken from this world.

She had never been more scared in her life. She knew a tentative plan lay in place, but the gist of it was to make it to the computers connecting the machine that made up the central A.I. and destroy the system in whatever way possible.

She knew they weren't entirely alone; Pro, the rebel android who made it back had managed to secure contact with a few other androids who populated the city, and were not enslaved to Cerberus. They planned to join up to fight together with the Stormwalkers, to whatever end may come.

Bastion mentioned a way to hack into the system Cerberus worked out of, but it was so far unknown how to crack. He and

Pro had been working on some kind of code all night, but they wouldn't know it to be successful until they stood within reach of those specific computer systems. Bastion would need to plug in to the system, if only for a few seconds, to upload the code into Cerberus' mainframe. That was the extent of Nemo's knowledge of it. Computers and technology of the Old World still confused her at times. But she knew it to be their only hope, therefore it was paramount it succeeds.

As long as the Stormwalkers and the rebels could hold everything off long enough for Bastion to get to the computers, nothing else would matter. At least, she had to think that way. If she began to believe it wouldn't work, they wouldn't stand a chance. There'd be no escaping the city, and if not outright killed, they'd live a life of certain misery.

She rolled over, a sigh escaping her. There was no way she would sleep tonight. She didn't know why she even bothered trying.

"Nemo?" a voice whispered.

She couldn't tell at first if it was Bastion or Aiden, which made her want to both laugh and cry. She and Aiden hadn't spoken in a friendly manner since they had fought. Was he trying to reach out before they walked into almost certain death?

She rolled back over to see who had whispered her name, but it was not Aiden. It was Bastion.

"Can't sleep?" he asked.

"Of course not. How could I, knowing tomorrow we could all be dead?"

"You've fought in many battles prior to this. Are you not used to this by now?" he attempted a joke.

"I would think so," she said. "But so much is different now. I just don't know."

"Alright, I'm sorry. Is there anything I can do?"

"Not really. I... I'm... upset... about Hobbes and Gord. I can't get the thought of them out of my mind. That, and Aiden and I fought and it's just an inconvenient time for it. There's a chance one or both of us won't come out of there alive. And how could I live with myself if I survive this, and he doesn't? Then I'll have lost three great friends, without being able to save any of them. I would hate myself if Aiden died, and we never made up. And now I'm rambling."

"So make up with him," Bastion stated. "Tell him it's a stupid time to be fighting and you're wrong, or he's wrong or whatever you have to say. Don't let pride or whatever get in the way, because you're right. One or both of you may not get the chance later, and that'll be that. Not getting to say goodbye, not getting to express how important they are to you before they're gone, it's awful, Nemo. I know it."

"You would, I know. You're right, it's just... I don't know. I'm stubborn, I guess. And he is too. And we are terrible at admitting we're wrong, even if it's true."

"Then try to get some sleep. You need rest before tomorrow. Try not to worry about anything else tonight."

"Easy for you to say... but thank you. I wish... I wish we didn't judge you so harshly before," she muttered.

"I get it. It's alright," he said, softly. "But thank you."

"I'm so grateful to have you here, Bastion." she said, rolling back over. "Goodnight."

"Goodnight, Nemo."

Nemo tried her best to let sleep take her, laying restlessly for hours before settling into the darkness.

Aiden laid down for sleep early. He knew there'd be a tough time falling asleep; he always had trouble sleeping knowing a battle lay ahead. There was the fear he would lose friends--in this case, practically family--in the process of fighting for what they believed in. He knew it to be a part of war, but it was a part he hated. It was a dream that increasingly came true, which was something no amount of his training as a Stormwalker could prepare him for.

He lay there in his bed, sending out wishes to whoever might be listening; *Please keep Nemo alive. Please keep Deacon alive. Please even keep Bastion alive.* He knew it to be a long shot, but he didn't know what else to do. He couldn't lose anyone else, least of all Nemo.

He sat and thought about what he would do if Nemo didn't make it, a thought trail he had followed before. And just like before, the results would be tragic and devastating.

He hoped beyond anything their plan would somehow provide some sort of miracle where they would come out victorious. They didn't have any options left. They needed this win.

Please let this work.

After a while, he heard Nemo and Bastion settle into their respective sleeping spots, hoping to find some comfort in sleep as well. While Bastion was rather stationary and silent, Nemo proved quite the opposite. She flopped from side to side, making creaking noises each time she turned over. It would be enough to keep anyone up, but Aiden knew Nemo always had a hard time sleeping knowing there was a very good chance someone could die soon. He knew her well enough to know it bothered her, and she wouldn't sleep well for most of the night.

At some point, Bastion must have decided he'd had enough

of listening to her rustle about, as he whispered to her. Aiden couldn't make out most of the words, and he honestly didn't want to pry, but he could tell Bastion tried to comfort her, tell her to get some sleep, and the advice proved useless. He knew better than anyone she would fall asleep only when her body couldn't sustain being awake any longer, only then would she let herself succumb to sleep.

As Bastion tried to offer words of comfort and jokes, she shut him down, which raised Aiden's spirits slightly. It made him feel like he had one up on Bastion, a preposterous thought to have. He reminded himself the two were not in competition, but sometimes it sure seemed like he competed for Nemo's attention lately. He shook the thought out of his head, his ears perking up at the mention of his name.

She was upset about their fight, and wanted to make up. His heart melted a bit at the thought, particularly when she mentioned how devastated she would be if one or both of them ended up dead, and they never made up. He was further surprised by Bastion's suggestion of making it right with him. He didn't expect that at all. Perhaps he and the cyborg might find a way to get along after all. But he knew how stubborn both he and Nemo could be, and resigned that in the morning, he would apologize to her. He would say he was wrong, that he shouldn't have started a fight, and they would make up before they went to war. It was the only way.

The two said goodnight, and a long time before Aiden heard Nemo's rustlings end as she finally fell asleep. He allowed himself to drift off as well, hoping to see her in his dreams.

Morning arrived; it had been a long time coming, considering the fitful rest most had. The group gathered together, once more going over their thoughts on what was to come, talking about tactic and approach. A lot of what would be on the fly, last minute decision-making.

"Nemo, could I talk to you for a minute?" Aiden asked, as they got ready to take off.

Nemo stepped over, looking ready to take orders.

"I just wanted to say I'm sorry for yesterday. I'm sorry we fought; I shouldn't have let my emotions get hold of me like they did. Hobbes and Gord---it's been hard to take and I... I wasn't there. I let it get to me and I took it out on you and that was wrong of me. I'm sorry."

Nemo didn't say a word. Instead, she wrapped her arms around him, holding him in a bear hug. The gesture said more than words ever would. He pulled back, looking her in the eye.

"Thank you, Aiden," she said with a smile. "I know things are different. And I don't know where we will end up from here, but know you are important. To me. To all of us."

He nodded. He also didn't know where they would end up moving forward, but right there, right now, he was happy with this.

"We're going to make it out of this," he promised, knowing full well it to be bad practice to do so. "It's time."

The group trekked their way back to the central A.I., to the place of all their woes. That's the only way Aiden could think of it now. He felt he owed it to Hobbes and Gord to think of it as a way to remember the place. He needed some sort of marker, be it physical or only in Aiden's head.

Soon, they were back in place; Cerberus lay in their sights

once again. For now, no other androids surrounded to protect it. Aiden thought this was strange, but imagined the room could be full of androids in seconds. They really did react like a beehive. If they were going to do this, they would need to move quickly.

"Bastion, are you ready?"

Bastion glanced over at Nemo. She nodded at him once, telling him it was okay, that it was time to do this.

"Yes, I think so," he said, sounding unsure. He looked to Pro. The two needed to work together to get to the computer system, while Nemo, Aiden, and the others fought off the waves of androids that were bound to show up.

"Okay, move. We'll hold them off as much as we can. You sure the code you got will do the trick?" Aiden asked.

Pro nodded. "Affirmative. This unit has worked with the cyborg Bastion to develop a worm code. As long as this unit or Bastion can access the terminal on Cerberus' main hub, the worm can be introduced. An algorithm will then work its own way into the central A.I.'s subroutines and eliminate Cerberus' virulent code."

"There is something else Pro isn't mentioning," Bastion said.

The group looked at him, incredulous. Now was not the time for last minute problems.

"If we succeed--if this code works--Cerberus will be destroyed, but so might all the androids working under its control. These androids aren't bad, Aiden. They can't help it. Because they are slaved to Cerberus' command codes, there is a possibility they will be destroyed as well. Anything that is connected to the system will go down. For all I know, my own cybernetic systems may fail. We couldn't find a workaround."

Nemo panicked. "You never mentioned that before!"

"I am sorry. I knew you would have demanded another way. We don't have the time. Not anymore."

Aiden gritted his teeth, thinking. "It's a risk we're gonna have to take. I'm sorry, but Bastion is right. We don't have time to come up with something else."

"We aren't finished, Bastion" Nemo said without confidence. "I'll make a Stormwalker out of you yet."

Bastion nodded, "Okay. I promise to live up to that."

Aiden said, "Okay, are we ready?"

"No. But let's do this," she replied, gripping her staff.

Deacon and Larina nodded their readiness, and Aiden realized their time had come.

It was time to end it.

Bastion and Pro took off, sprinting in the direction of the computer systems, while the others split off in opposite directions. It barely took a minute for Cerberus' defenses to activate, and slaved androids entered the labs. But Pro signaled to indicate many of the units present were the promised remaining rebels, which served to balance the numbers, if even just slightly.

The scene that laid out before them was very similar to the day before. Aiden couldn't help but feel a sense of déja vu. The familiar waves of enemies began again, and he took down each android that came before him, knocking them down one at a time.

Aiden knew they had to break the routine.

Bastion and Pro sprinted as fast as they could, making a beeline for the computer system. They also had to fend off constant oncoming attackers, but soon reached the hub of the central A.I. platform. Pro pulled out a cord and connected Bastion via his cybernetic eye to the computer system.

"It will take about a minute, perhaps longer, for the worm program to upload," Pro said. "You must remain connected for the transfer to succeed. This unit will defend your position."

The upload began. Pro stood guard, using a borrowed Stormwalker sidearm to strike down its fellow androids who got too close. Meanwhile, Bastion waited as the percentage meter on the screen ticked up one number at a time, listening to the sounds of battle around him. He tried not to think about Nemo struggling to fight for her life, but the picture came to mind, anyway.

While the chaos ensued, Nemo spotted movement above them. Glancing up, she witnessed the mechanical form of Cerberus twist in its place, and for the first time, raise its arms.

"Organic intruders have infiltrated Cerberus systems," Cerberus droned loudly outward to her minions. "Makers' prerogatives compromised! Destroy all organics!"

Soon, piles of androids lay at Bastion's feet. Pro fired again, but the clip clicked empty. The android threw the gun at another attacker, and charged into the crowd. The android used its own fists, swinging again and again to fend off the metallic mob. But soon, Pro was swallowed up in the mass of its own fellow robots.

98%, 99%, 100%. Bastion unplugged himself and joined the fray. He swung, jumped, struck, raced around the lab. He far outpaced the android bodies, but they had numbers on their side. Even with the aid of the remaining rebels, his cybernetic systems instantly calculated probable failure once again, unless the worm did its job.

It seemed like the fight would never end. Bastion saw an android swipe at Nemo, dropping her to her knees. He ran in her direction, knowing that one fell swoop would end her life before he would ever reach her.

And then all the violence and mayhem was drowned out as Cerberus let out a viscous scream.

An infinite moment passed for Nemo as she witnessed the android's weapon fall slowly toward her, her eyes wide as her life flashed before them. But then, the weapon stopped, the android attacker frozen in place. It was as if the robot suddenly become confused with what it was doing. It shuddered a moment, then stood straight.

The fighting all around them ceased, and Bastion's head whipped to look at the hub of Cerberus. The computer screens were frying, and the being that was hooked up to the system looked to be shorting out. The body of the artificial being known as Cerberus convulsed again and again. Its hands clutched the sides of its platform with a death grip, cracking concrete and cables into dust. Lights flickered, Cerberus let out a mechanical, hollow groan, and the room lit up in a wave of cascading energy that shot its way through every android present. Darkness followed.

Silence.

They had done it; they had stopped Cerberus and the androids stopped fighting. The control Cerberus had over this synthetic city was over. The rebels won. The Stormwalkers had won.

The androids were free.

Bastion was still self-aware. That was a good start. He checked his own systems, and found that though they suffered slight corrosion from the energy burst, he functioned fine. He looked around to see Nemo and the other Stormwalkers still standing. A wave of relief washed over him, knowing they were all safe. As she struggled back to her feet, he viewed Aiden come to her aid. They stood side by side, and as Bastion watched them, he was happy.

But then everyone noticed the still-standing androids did just that; standing still and straight and lifeless. Bastion and Pro had been right. In destroying Cerberus, they ended the existence of all the androids.

CHAPTER TWENTY SEVEN

Aiden looked around at the frozen army of androids. The fight was over. Although elated this meant Cerberus defeated for good, it pained him to realize Bastion and Pro had been right.

He looked over to Nemo, just so glad for her to be alright. He had done all he could to fix their relationship, he apologized and told her how important she was to him, but he now knew things were going to be as they were meant to be.

And then a movement jarred him from his thoughts of jealousy. A single android, off to his right, tilted its head in a spasm. Then its shoulders. Then a flex of fingers. He then spotted another android do the same, followed by another. And another. The androids begun to move again, only this time, they did not reach for their weapons. They did not make any sudden movements. They looked around, appeared confused or lost, as if under a spell for a long time.

He waited as they gathered together, sounding rather frightened, and tried to learn what each of the other robots remembered. He prepared to make an announcement, but Bastion beat him to it.

"Many of you will be confused," the cyborg started. "You have been under the control of the central A.I. -- Cerberus -- the program which took control of this entire city, for many years. You have been following an ancient control order, to capture and experiment on any human specimen you came into contact with. You stored their DNA profiles in your labs, you did harmful tests, and you created me as I stand before you now. All of which, the intent is unclear. These were the directives of your makers. We don't know where the information came from, but Cerberus followed its objectives from this computer system, that is now destroyed."

The androids looked around at each other, taking Bastion's word as revelation.

"Does anybody remember anything from their time under Cerberus' control?" Pro's voice spoke out. He emerged from the crowd, hobbling into view. Both his arms had been torn off, exposing severed wires and dripping bluish fluids. One of his feet was also missing, making it difficult for him to balance on his own legs. "Though we won this battle, we are not finished here. We have been able to stop Cerberus from harming our human friends, but the protocols did not end there."

A small hand rose above the crowd. Bastion pointed to the android, waiting to learn what information this robot would give.

"There's a hangar bay. At the city's outskirts," a short female-looking android said. "Where one would store a large vehicle. This unit was assigned the location to perform routine mainte-nance. This unit believes it remembers how to return. This unit is not aware of what the significance of it is, but the file is high-lighted, therefore must be of importance."

"Good, take us there."

This android led the way for the robots and the Stormwalkers to follow. They traipsed through the maze of Building 234, through hallways Aiden and his companions had never seen or entered before, and soon out into the city.

As they journeyed through the streets, Aiden was amazed how different he viewed it all compared to their arrival. Back then, he'd no idea of the hidden agendas, the deceit, the danger. But now, he watched as android units greeted each other and conversed with renewed sense of purpose. The city had been a prison when they arrived. Now, it would be a home again.

After a pleasant walk in even more pleasant weather, they stood in front of what appeared to be another massive building, not unlike the city center's Building 234. This building had large open spaces surrounding it, with cracked pavement encircling the building that served for vehicle transport long ago. It all reminded Aiden of a certain area back at Safe Harbor, where they believed the Stormmakers once housed great flying machines that reached for the stars. It was how he originally met Nemo, finding her in a supposedly downed airplane, and the thought pained him. But he pushed the thought aside as the group entered the premises.

They found a row of buildings, hangars that once served as storage for airplanes. They found a couple of decayed planes stored within, similar to the one he and Hobbes met her in; the one called The Nemo, of which he nicknamed her after. That was so long ago now.

Those thoughts threatened their return again, but halted as the group came upon an especially large hangar building. They entered through the side door, to find a massively cavernous space; this was not just a garage for the regular planes. This was something else entirely. Aiden noticed there didn't seem to be a large enough door for the vehicle to enter, making this room more confusing.

"How do the vehicles enter?" he asked.

"Uh, Aiden...?" Larina said, pointing up.

There appeared to be a large opening overhead. If designed to be the entryway for a flying machine, it was a massive plane indeed. The android that led them to the garage pushed a button on a panel, and the skylight retracted, leaving a larger opening in the ceiling.

"That'd be a huge airplane," Aiden said.

"This unit remembers now," the android stated. "They came from the skies. They had flying vehicles, and so they would enter through the ceiling. It was this unit's role to ensure safe landings."

"They?" Nemo asked.

"Yes, they," Bastion said. "Like we discovered; Cerberus took its orders from a higher power. That higher power, whoever they are, came here in flying vehicles."

"The Stormmakers," Deacon muttered.

"The Makers traveled here long ago," said Pro. "They were our masters, our creators. Where did they go?"

Aiden wandered around the edges of the hangar, looking at what kind of technology filled its space. There were many computer screens and servers, more than those connected to Cerberus, which Aiden found rather curious. If the central A.I. was supposed to be the main hub of the city, why would the Stormmakers need even more computing power just for travel purposes?

"So, now what?" Larina questioned.

"For the first time," Pro announced, "we are free. We thank you, Stormwalkers."

Aiden nodded. "What's your next move then, Pro? Does this place help you to understand a purpose for you and your people?"

"The mysteries of the Makers continue," the android replied. "We may never understand what our creators were like, but we now know the orders we received were wrong and obsolete."

Bastion started to speak, but paused. He thought back to the memory archives he briefly saw earlier. *Should I tell them? Are they ready for that?*

"We are free now," Pro continued. "Free to choose."

"To choose?"

"You Stormwalkers mentioned before of your own mission; venturing into the numerous eyes of the Storms that cover our world, finding those who need help, and helping them. This unit believes you stated the home you call Safe Harbor as being open to new members?"

"That's right. Are you saying you'll join us?"

"This unit is saying-"

A colossal boom of sound blasted down upon them as if from the heavens. It was deeper, and shook his bones harder than anything any raging Storm had ever sent Aiden's way. It practically paralyzed him.

And he wasn't the only one. Everyone in the room struggled to remain on their feet as the roar hit them from above, and in that monumental moment, Aiden dared to look up.

A large aircraft lowered itself through the skylight, covered in flashing lights. The vehicle was circular, disc-like, giving off repeated pulses of light as it lowered itself closer and closer.

Soon it came to rest, hovering above the ground without the need for landing gear.

Aiden and the others were on the edge of their seats, waiting to see who or what would exit the vehicle. But if they thought to get a view, they were sadly mistaken. A sound like a can opening--a sort of hissing sound-- filled the air, and suddenly a bright light illuminated the room. The light, so intense, so all-encompassing, that anyone who didn't squeeze their eyes tight immediately felt harsh burning. But even with eyes closed, it felt as though the light was actually trying to rip its way through their eyelids to burn everything away.

"Keep your eyes closed!" Aiden yelled to everyone, but even as he did so, he realized he couldn't hear his own voice, drowned out completely by the monstrous roar of the aircraft. Was it the ship's motor? What else could it be?

After several minutes, the light finally faded, and it took a minute for their eyes to adjust to the growing darkness of the hangar.

It was clear, by the time their eyes adjusted, that their guests--whoever they might have been--had gone. The craft was gone. The light was gone. It was empty. Silence. Looking up, all they saw was the twinkling of stars in the night sky.

"Night?!" Deacon said. "Where did the day go?"

"You're right," Aiden realized. "Daylight just a few minutes ago."

"What do we do now?" Nemo wondered, looking at Bastion.

"That is a good question..." Bastion trailed off. What just happened here?

"Who in the world travels in something like that?" Aiden asked.

"I always thought the Stormmakers fell," Bastion said. "I

thought they would have crumbled to nothing, what with the world the way it is. Have they been hiding somewhere else all this time? Have they only grown since the world fell?"

Aiden had no answer. He, too, always believed the Storm-makers to be figures of history. He never once imagined they would still exist somewhere in the world, alive and active. But if so, it terrified him to picture a direct encounter with them.

"Hey, is that computer turned on?" Nemo pointed over to one of the many computer screens.

She was right. Despite the darkness, and presumably everything shutting down, there was one screen that had been left on. They cautiously made their way over to the computer to see what was left on the screen, to learn if there was anything to point them in the direction of who or what they might be dealing with.

The screen was mostly black, but with a line of written code blinking against its dark backdrop.

Chaidh casg a chur air cruinneachadh dàta. Pròiseact Gàradh air a chuir an cunnart. Thòisich Failsafes. Tòisich an glanadh deireannach. Tòisichidh ath-chuairteachadh.

Aiden turned to Nemo in the gloom, and all he could make out was her wide-eyed stare.

"No," she whispered.

The group stood at the bridge leading out of the city. Their gear packed, they were ready for the journey ahead.

Aiden approached Pro. The android had since received a new pair of arms, and he reached one out as a gesture for Aiden. The young Stormwalker took the android's hand in his and gave a firm shake.

"It's been an adventure," he said to the robot city's new leader. "Can't say I'd like to do it again."

Pro nodded. "Much was lost in getting here. On both sides. But we are free now, and this unit has learned there are many choosing to make the journey to Safe Harbor in the times ahead."

"We've shown you the way. You'll be welcome."

"We will be sending a representative for us in the meantime, to get things started with your people. This unit believes you are already acquainted with him."

A single android approached, and indeed Aiden recognized the robot; Uka, the very first android they'd encountered in the swamps, which had led them down the strange and winding path of this journey.

"Uka, I'm glad you're joining us," he told the android.

"Uka Five-Two-Zero-Zero is this unit's proper designation," Uka said.

"Right, of course."

"But this unit is also glad to be joining you. This unit looks forward to building a future at your Safe Harbor."

"It's your Safe Harbor too," Aiden said as he shook Pro's hand a final time. "All of yours."

Pro nodded. "Good luck, Stormwalker."

The group turned and crossed the bridge. Before long, they were well into the swamp and the signs of the android city were far behind them.

The group walked in silence, with only the occasional mention of their surroundings. Eventually though, Aiden spoke up, directing his thoughts to Nemo and Deacon.

"I still have a lot to learn of the Stormwalker tongue, but I recognize the writing when I see it. Why was the Stormwalker language written on that computer screen? What did it say?"

Nemo remained quiet. Aiden could tell from looking at her she was at battle with thoughts flowing through her mind. Did she know something?

Deacon sighed. "I can't tell you why it was on that screen. I wish I knew. This makes little sense. But I can tell you, based on what it said, we need to get back to Safe Harbor. The faster the better. We need to warn the Stormwalkers."

"Warn them of what? What did we see in that hangar? What did it say?"

Deacon sighed again. "The rough translation; Data collection stopped. Project 'Garden' compromised. Fail safes initiated, cleansing to commence."

"Project...what?! What fail safe? What cleansing?"

"I don't know. We must hurry. Everything has changed."

"Should we be worried?" Aiden pleaded. "Why do we need to be afraid of the Stormmakers?"

"Those weren't the Stormmakers," Nemo said with a shudder.

Aiden looked at her incredulously. But she marched onward, and Deacon simply regarded his son.

Then Nemo and Deacon picked up their pace. Aiden glanced to Bastion and Larina, both of whom shrugged. What was happening here? What did the two original Stormwalkers know the others did not?

Aiden didn't understand this sudden turn of events. Just hours ago, despite the cost, they achieved a great victory. Now, a foreboding blanket of mystery enveloped them. And he didn't appreciate both his friend and his father seemed to have an idea of it while keeping the rest of them in the dark. He looked to Bastion again, and as he shared a look with the former Eagle he came to realize they would have something common to work toward. He and the cyborg would need to get to the bottom of this together, whatever end it led to.

And thus, a small group of adventurers comprising four Stormwalkers, an android, and a cyborg, continued their journey through the wilds, toward a return to a familiar home, and an uncertain future.

THE SKY BLARED with the trumpets of noise brought on by the power of the Storm. The Storm Wall, which reached far across the horizon, continued its swirling maelstrom of power, an ever-present force revered by its inhabitants for generations. Those inhabitants feared the Storm, and greater still, feared the notion of what might exist within that Storm. Their reverence, brought to levels of religious fervor through the ages, kept most of them willfully within the Storm's Eye. Most of them were content to remain inside. Most, but not all.

It was a shock when news spread some people were plotting to seek a place outside the Eye that would sustain them. The sheer blasphemy of it shook the entire Eye. When the first time came that a group of inhabitants decided they had had enough of the swirling maelstrom, they left with a suicidal quest to find a better land for everyone to dwell. And even though no one was happy about their venture into the unknown, the hope of a haven outside the Eye made everyone buy into their presence for escape.

They were never seen again.

But their cause had been right. The remaining inhabitants discovered the maps that showed their Eye would lose its ground, and the sea would be their doom. So they prayed for the courage those first voyagers had, and they made their own choice. They made a choice their leader despised right to his very bones.

A group of figures emerged from the Storm, blindly making their way one foot at a time. Their clothing covered their features. Rags and wrapping protected their faces, blinding them from the world around them, but allowed them to painstakingly eke their way forward.

Eventually the group came to a pause at the crest of a sand dune. The Stormwall behind them, they allowed themselves a moment of respite.

The group consisted of a few dozen individuals, all clad in robes and goggles and masks, and whatever else they could use to force their way through the Storm. Ahead of the group three individuals stood, and although their clothing pieces differed, each piece was dyed the same uniform color of purple. An etched glyph of a powerful bird was displayed on each of their chest pieces.

The glyph of an Eagle.

As the nomads began to settle for air and rest, one of the three eagle-robed figures pulled off their mask to reveal a young woman of bronzed skin and dark hair. She shook her scrunched hair free and allowed a thick braid to cascade down to the middle of her back. She wiped her face with her hands, revealing her hands were shackled together, her wrists bound in rope. The woman turned to the leader of the group.

As he pulled a scarf away, their leader revealed a face well into his later years, though he still held a hard edge that resonated power which was only momentarily betrayed by his tired eyes. The man's body suddenly jerked as he coughed into a purple scrap of cloth, his aged visage coming away to reveal spots of blood on the material. He glared at it a moment, until the third purple-robed nomad pulled his goggles off and faced him.

He was the youngest of the three by far, his freckled face revealing an age of no more than a teenager, with his red hair haphazardly sliced short as if with a dull blade. His green eyes flashed with vigor as he stared at the older man and the coughed-up blood. "Lord Jorus, please steady yourself. You can't take much more of this."

Jorus regarded the young man, then simply nodded. "Do not worry, my young apprentice. We've come too far for me to fall now. This old Eagle has some fight in him still."

A scoff from the young woman drew Jorus' attention.

"Something you find amusing?" the old man asked.

"Sure do," she replied. "The sight of an old man trying to convince his new puppet and himself that he's a god and not just a withering shell really makes a good joke."

Jorus chuckled. "Still bitter, I see. Well, my little Canary, that anger will serve you well if you wish to survive what lay ahead of us."

"You won't find them." Canary declared. "Not after all this time. This is all for nothing."

"Do not question Lord Jorus," the young man rebuked.

"It's alright." Jorus said. "Canary is afraid. We all are. Now that we have seen what is coming, I don't blame her."

"Even If we do find them, do you think it'll be enough?"

Jorus reached into his robe and withdrew a pair of battered binoculars. He turned back the way they came, and lifted the lenses to his eyes, shifting the focus until satisfied. At first, all he saw was the wall of the Storm they'd gotten through. But he knew it was in there, somewhere. They had seen it. They had escaped it.

There. He could just make out the faintest presence of it within the Storm. That unmistakable shape. It was massive. Curved angles, claws that reached ever outward, and a gaping maw filled with unending rows of rotating teeth.

Oh, it was still out there.

It was still after them.

"I don't know," Jorus muttered. "But we need all the help we can get. We need Deacon. We need the Stormwalkers. Or we are all doomed."

AFTERWORD

Well, if you made it this far I'm assuming you enjoyed the story! If that's the case, I've a favour to ask. Please, please, please take a moment to leave a review. It doesn't have to be elaborate, just a few words is plenty! They go a long way to help writers gain readers, and just think, the book's success would in part be due to your own hand. Pretty cool, no?

Leave a review on AMAZON today!

Or leave a review on GOODREADS!

Thanks again, and just you wait; there are more adventures to come…

ABOUT THE AUTHOR

R.K.King is a writer of novels, screenplays and short fiction. When not writing or reading, he enjoys movies, video games and being a well-rounded nerd. He lives in British Columbia with his wife and cat. Get a FREE short story and keep up to date by joining the RK King Readers' Tribe at rkkingwrites.com